The *Christmas Spirit*

LOU AGUILAR

To Dave, Sharon, & Jaydin,
Merry Christmas 2020.

Lou Aguilar

This is a work of fiction. Names, characters, places, and incidents are products of the author's imagination or are used fictitiously and are not to be construed as real. Any resemblance to actual events, locations, organizations, or persons, living or dead, is entirely coincidental.

World Castle Publishing, LLC
Pensacola, Florida

Copyright © Lou Aguilar 2020
Paperback ISBN: 9781953271303
eBook ISBN: 9781953271310
First Edition World Castle Publishing, LLC, November 16, 2020
http://www.worldcastlepublishing.com

Licensing Notes

Cover: Karen Fuller
Editor: Maxine Bringenberg

Chapter One

Given the festive occasion—the *Sublime Magazine* Christmas party aboard the cruise boat Voyager 2—Caroline York tried to fake jubilance. But the champagne and generic Christmas music only added to her melancholy. Her group of four had commandeered the small sitting area in the lounge, two beige sofas facing each other across a white vinyl roundtable next to a portside window. Out the window, she could see the Maine coast lights two miles west. Beyond her group, twenty-three elegant people, just two over age forty, drank, chatted, flirted, and flattered Executive Editor Rita Lyton, sixty-three years old yet unwrinkled as iron.

Caroline focused on the three people closest to her. Beside her sat her rich lawyer fiancé, Peter Fleming, brown hair perfectly coiffed to hide the small bald spot on top. Mustached black editor Paul Scott and his cheerful wife, Ann, occupied the other couch. All were sipping Dom Perignon, the now empty bottle on the table. Caroline tried to tune in their conversation so she could seamlessly rejoin it. Fortunately for her, a pretty Indian waitress distracted them, bearing a tray of hors d'oeuvre. Each of them plucked a snack.

Paul bit into his first and made an appreciative face. "Delicious caviar snack," he said, turning to Ann. "You should make these at home."

"I'll be happy to, dear, after you get your Christmas bonus."

"What Christmas bone—?"

Paul shut up, seeing Ann and Caroline smiling at him. He joined them.

"This party is our bonus," said Caroline. "It's as generous as Rita gets once a year."

"I forget," said Paul. "We only cover the rich and famous — from the cheap seats."

"Speak for yourself, Paul," said Peter, sampling his snack. "Caroline will always have the place of honor in my orchestra box."

He placed his right hand over the large diamond on Caroline's ring finger, eliciting a wan smile from her.

"I knew I should've gone into law instead of journalism," Paul said.

"You might win an argument with our five-year-old sometime," said Ann.

"Rory's five already?" said Caroline. "Good lord."

"Time flies," Ann said. "How long have you two been going now?"

"Nine months and three weeks," answered Peter.

"Ever since we featured him in *Sublime*," said Paul. "Peter Fleming, Attorney to the Stars."

"Caroline made me seem irresistible. Yet she still won't set the date."

"What are you waiting for, Caroline?"

inquired Ann.

Caroline paused for a moment before answering. "I don't know. A little mystery perhaps, before settling down for good."

"Like where did my UNC sweatshirt disappear to," said Paul.

Ann made a flamboyant "search me" gesture, garnering smiles.

Caroline turned serious. "I mean it, though. The lifestyle we're paid to promote—film, fashion, food, and—"

"Frolic," Paul said.

"It's all rather superficial, isn't it?" Caroline noticed Peter's frown and caressed his right wrist with her free hand. "Present company excepted," she said. "I'd like to write about something more…extraordinary for a change."

"Well, 'tis the season," Ann said.

"To be jolly, not heavy," said Paul, wiggling his empty champagne glass. "What's holding up our refill?"

"I'll grab us a bottle," Caroline said, standing up. "And I promise to be appropriately festive the rest of the night." She winked and went to the bar.

"Dom Perignon," she told the middle-aged Indian bartender. "Bottle, please."

He placed one in front of her.

"I was hoping to return those at half price," said a haughty female voice behind her. "The cheaper brand only pays one third."

Caroline turned to face Rita Lyton, as usual, like a novice before the Mother Superior. "So I've ruined your reputation as Mrs. Scrooge," said Caroline.

"Bah humbug," said Rita. "I'd have divorced Ebenezer for being too generous."

Caroline chuckled. Rita nodded at the bottle in her employee's hand. "Don't let it go to your head, Caroline. I still want that Congresswoman Hartley piece by Friday." She moved away toward her circle of sycophants.

Caroline clutched the bottle. "I hope she's paying you enough," she said to the bartender.

He pointed at a bill-filled goblet on the bar. "My daughter and I get tips," he said with a faint Indian accent. "Unlike the ship's crew."

"Oh? How many are there?"

"On this charter, five men, including Captain Fowler."

Caroline looked at the bottle in her hand, getting an idea. "Some expensive bubbly might compensate them. Do me a favor, will you? Send another bottle to that drunken lot over there." She pointed to her sitting group.

"Of course."

Caroline moved to the lounge exit and took the three steps to the door. Cold air struck her the instant she opened it, aided by her short, sleeveless, velvet cocktail dress. Her high heels and slight buzz made walking the portside deck a bit tricky, so she took full advantage of the handrail. She saw dark waves rolling away from the ship and a beam of light sweeping the ocean ahead.

Reaching the pilothouse, she found the door locked and minus a doorbell. She knocked three times. The door swung open, held by a robust, handsome senior with a trim grey beard in a captain's uniform, sans cap. "Well, blow me down," he said in a noticeable Maine accent. "A mermaid."

"I have legs," said Caroline.

"And lovely ones too, but you're barely standing on 'em. Come on in."

Captain Fowler opened the door wider. Caroline stepped into a high-tech bridge dominated by a lofty chair behind the ivory mariner wheel. The curving front window offered a wide view of the dark sea ahead. The captain indicated a wooden chest on the starboard side.

"Sit."

Caroline sat on the chest.

"What can I do for you, missy?"

Caroline held out the bottle. "Christmas present for you and your crew."

Captain Fowler smirked. "Champagne. Never touch the stuff. Now rum — that'd be different."

"Oh," said Caroline. "I'll go get you some."

"I'm joking, missy. We don't touch booze while at sea. Your landlubber lives depend on us staying sharp. For instance, I see you're not wearing a life jacket. Didn't you hear the first mate's castoff speech? Life vest on deck at all times."

"I left mine by my coat."

"Foolish girl, 'specially tonight."

"Why tonight, especially?"

"There be whales," said Captain Fowler. "All around. Sometimes they rock the boat."

"Whales, wow. Could I see one?"

"Possibly, from the deck."

"I'll go tell my friends," said Caroline, rising to her feet.

"Not without a vest. Grab one from that chest."

Caroline lifted the trunk lid and extracted an orange lifejacket. She put the champagne down on the reclosed chest so she could don the vest. She struggled with the straps for half a minute, to the captain's amusement, and had to take a break.

"Can't I just carry it?" she asked.

Captain Fowler shook his head. "Too dangerous. You're not a real mermaid."

"As if there are any."

"Oh, there are."

"Right," said Caroline, again fumbling with

the straps. "Ever see one?"

"That I have."

Caroline looked at Captain Fowler. "Oh, come on."

"Sail the seas long enough, missy, and you'll spy things you never dreamed could be. Marvelous things. I plan to write a book about it someday when I'm dry-docked for good. But I might need a ghostwriter. Ha ha."

"I would like to review your book," said Caroline. "Look me up, will you? Caroline York, *Sublime Magazine*, Boston."

"I just might do that. Thank you."

Caroline finally clicked on the vest. She pointed to the champagne bottle on the trunk. "For your wife," she said.

"She was hardier than me."

"Oh, sorry."

"And you're nicer than most swells," Captain Fowler said. "Merry Christmas, mermaid."

Caroline exited the pilothouse, the lifejacket a new layer against the cold, her clearer head counterbalancing the high heels. She moved aft with no need for rail support.

Halfway to the lounge door, a loud, mournful wail froze her in her tracks. *There be whales*, she recalled.

She rushed to the handrail and leaned over it. She scanned the ocean surface, which was brightened by the beam she'd seen earlier, now passing closer to the ship. She could make out its point of origin—an old-style lighthouse on a small island maybe half a mile away. A nearer movement distracted her, a massive shadow disappearing underneath the vessel. The deck rocked then fell seaward, flipping Caroline over the handrail. A blast of water cut off her scream.

Chapter Two.

Caroline thrashed in the ocean for a good while before realizing she was still afloat, thanks to the lifejacket. She managed to turn around to where the cruise ship had been — and no longer was. Only open sea spanned before her. She heard a faint rendition of *I'll be Home for Christmas*. Turning left, she caught sight of the boat moving rapidly away. Her shouts of "No!" and "Stop!" blended with the fading music. By the time she quit yelling, the song could no longer be heard. She began to sob.

"God, help me," she prayed for the first time since childhood.

A beam of light shone down on her. It came not from Heaven but the lighthouse to her left. The island where it stood seemed so close, she thought she could swim to it, like Charlize Theron. "The women I play can do anything men can do, and better," Charlize had told her in an interview. It was time to prove her right. She began to swim with strong, swift strokes.

The light swept away, and darkness enveloped her, sapping her resolve. The cold bit into her. She swam as if the exercise would warm her, until she couldn't feel her arms. Her strokes slowed, then ceased. She looked ahead. The lighthouse seemed no closer. An icy wave splashed her back and kept rolling toward the island. She envied it. Her own forward motion had stopped for good. Up or down was the only movement that awaited her—in the afterlife. Down would be preferable, she thought, hell being hot and dry.

A new light caught her eye, smaller than the lighthouse beam, at sea level and approaching fast. She knew a hallucination when she saw one, and this fit the bill—a little sailboat with a square golden sail, piloted by a dark-haired, well-built man in a white Irish fisherman's sweater and khaki dockers. She disbelieved in him even as his sailboat sped toward her. It came to a stop a few feet away.

She had a sense of being lifted out of the water by her upper arms, although she couldn't feel them enough to be sure. Laid down on her back in the front of the boat, she saw the golden sail above her and the star-filled sky beyond. A thick blanket dropped on her chest, held by the sailor, his face close and clear in the starlight. It didn't belong to a denizen from below…more of the higher realm—late twenties, handsome, with short brown hair and a square jaw darkened by stubble.

The face withdrew, restoring her view of the sail as it billowed with wind. The boat began to move. She watched the stars for an incalculable time, half expecting to float up to them at any moment. A slight jolt brought her back to Earth.

The attractive face reappeared just above hers. Strong hands dug into her back, beneath the lifejacket, and lifted her out of the sailboat.

She could see it was beached in a sandy cove between two large grey boulders, close to each other and illuminated by the lighthouse. The man carried her over the pebbly sand to between the twin rocks. The olden lighthouse loomed before them on the right shore. It was a grey-brick structure over a hundred feet high, crowned with a circular windowed station and ringed by a black metal walkway. *I made it*, thought Caroline, if only in her dying dream.

Chapter Three

They approached the lighthouse, the thick oaken door marked by a brass ring. The sailor pulled it open with one hand, the rest of both arms under Caroline, and bore her into the dimly lit structure. The bottom of a spiral black iron stairwell took up most of the ground floor. The man grabbed the smaller ring on the inside of the door and pulled it shut.

He began climbing the stairwell as if unburdened by the woman in his arms, made heavier by the thick blanket around her. Each flight looked identical, with a glassless arched window on the right revealing the sea. The sailor kept climbing rapidly. Even in a daze, Caroline regarded him with awe. He slowed down somewhat on the ninth level. Caroline could hear a male version of *Hark! The Herald Angels Sing* getting louder and clearer the higher they rose.

The twelfth flight emerged on a circular den lit by a hanging globe lamp. Caroline foggily took in the burgundy carpet, brown leather armchair, yellow sofa, pine coffee table, paperback-filled bookcase, plastic fireplace heater, combination washer-dryer, two-seat dinette table, and compact kitchen. A small music player atop the bookcase was playing the carol. On the false fireplace, mantel stood a miniature natural Christmas tree, oddly barren of any ornamentation. Two shut doors led, Caroline assumed, to the bathroom and bedroom, a sliding glass door to the outer deck. Through it, Caroline observed a silver telescope on a tripod, pointing at the ocean.

The sailor lay her down on the sofa and rushed to the artificial fireplace. He pressed a button on it, bringing the electric flame to life.

He returned to Caroline on the couch, with her groggily eying him. He cast off her blanket and smoothly unstrapped the lifejacket. He removed the vest but didn't stop there. He lowered the straps on her wet cocktail dress and pulled it down past her legs, exposing the black silk bra and panties meant for Peter's eyes only. She saw no hint of prurience on his face, only concern. He began vigorously rubbing her upper arms and thighs. The friction heat combined with the fireplace's to restore a tingling sensation to her body. The sailor nodded approvingly.

"Who are you?" she croaked.

"Name's Tate. Be right back."

He dashed to the left door and flicked a switch behind it. A ceiling light came on, revealing the bathroom. Caroline heard gushing water, mixed with a baritone version of *We Three Kings of Orient Are* on the stereo. Tate reappeared beside her. He scooped her up in his arms and carried her into the bathroom.

It was a narrow, windowless room with an antique bathtub elevated on four bronze bear legs. An attached rod held the optional showerhead and hose. Steam drifted up from the almost full tub. Tate gently lowered Caroline into it, feet at the faucet end. Hot water embalmed her. She leaned back and saw Tate leave the bathroom. She took off her underwear and closed her eyes.

When she reopened them, a blue cotton lady's robe hung on the door by the towel. She pondered if she could get to it or even out of the tub. Her arms proved strong enough, but when leaving the bathroom, her legs buckled, and she had to lean against the doorway for support.

She noticed the dinette table set for one on her side, with a tall glass of water and a white cloth napkin. A lovely rendition of *It Came Upon a Midnight Clear* played on the sound unit. Tate came out of the kitchen, holding a yellow mug, which he placed on the table. Spotting the unsteady Caroline in the doorway, he grimaced and dashed to her. He put his arm behind her back and helped her into the closer chair, then sat down in the other. Caroline looked at the wafting mug of chicken broth in front of her, then curiously at Tate. She noticed his brown eyes for the first time.

"You saved my life," she said.

"Just doing my job."

"How'd you...?" Caroline shivered, interrupting her own question.

Tate pointed to the mug. "Drink first. Then talk."

Caroline took a long sip of soup and wiped her lips. "How'd you get to me so fast?" she asked. "Not that I'm complaining, mind you."

Tate pointed to the glass door and the telescope beyond. "I was watching your boat go by. Saw you fall into the drink."

"The boat!" Caroline declared. "They'll think I'm dead. I need to use your phone."

"'Fraid I don't have one."

"Cellphone."

"Sorry."

"No cell? How do you communicate with the outside world?"

"I don't much," said Tate.

"What kind of lighthouse keeper are you?"

"I generally keep to myself. Where's your phone?"

"Obviously I lost it when I hit the—" Tate's knowing look shut her up. "I'm sorry, Tate. I know you saved me. It's just that—my friends'll be distraught."

"Then tomorrow they'll be overjoyed. Seeing you alive will be their Christmas joy."

"Can't you take me to the mainland tonight? I'll pay you."

"Sure, if you don't mind a few whale bumps along the way."

"Whales?" gulped Caroline.

"They're out there now. A whole school of them."

Caroline meekly sipped her broth.

"Look, you're alive, Miss…."

"York. Caroline."

"I've seen watery deaths, Caroline. They're pretty gruesome. Be thankful you were spared that fate. Use tonight to count your blessings and get a good night's sleep."

Caroline glanced around the small den. "Where?"

Tate pointed to the door on the right. "Bedroom."

"Ah. Where will you sleep?"

Tate pointed to the sofa.

Caroline nodded. "Thank you for looking after me."

"My pleasure."

"I doubt that," Caroline said with a slight smile. "I know I've been a pain in the rear."

"But easy on the eyes."

Caroline brushed her bathrobe. "Well, you have me at a disadvantage."

"Few men do, I'll bet," said Tate.

Caroline stared at his pleasing face. He looked past her at the glass door and frowned. She followed his eyes to the outside darkness. He stood up.

"Let's both get some rest," he said. "I'll need my strength to get you back to civilization in the morning." He pulled out Caroline's chair. She rose to her feet, steadier now. "There are more women's clothes in the closet."

"Oh?" said Caroline, as if expecting additional information.

"Take what you need for the voyage."

"Thank you."

"Good night," said Tate. "And Merry Christmas."

"It's not for four days."

"Oh, right. I got confused."

"See you in the morning," said Caroline.

Tate nodded.

Caroline walked into the bedroom. It was a cozy little room with a small window, an aluminum heater, presently off, a double bed draped by a brown comforter, a night table, a shaded lamp turned on, a dresser, a mirror, an antique desk set, and a closet. Caroline closed the door behind her and felt instantly colder. She tampered with the heater under the window sill until it came on. A memory flash struck her of Tate switching on the artificial fireplace. How could he have endured the cold before that? She looked out the window at the moonlit sea and shuddered as if it would reclaim her any moment.

She opened the closet door. Women's clothing took up most of it — grey sweatpants, a green flannel skirt, a purple ski jacket, pink and black T-shirts, white sneakers, and tan deck shoes. A man's olive green rain slicker hung on the right end. She wondered who Tate's female companion might be, and where. Moving to the bed, she removed her bathrobe. She got under the comforter and turned off the lamp. In two minutes, she was sound asleep.

A long wail broke her slumber. She recognized it in terror as the very sound she'd heard on the cruise boat right before she got thrown overboard. Just as she feared, she was still in the water. She thrashed, gasping for air as the dark ocean engulfed her.

"No!" she cried. "No!" Her sobs became screams. "Help! Help me!"

The bedroom door flew open. The bedside lamp came on, lighting Tate's face close to hers. His strong hands gripped her shoulders, providing instant warmth and the promise of safety. His calm voice seemed to validate the promise.

"It's all right, Caroline. You're safe."

Her shivering decreased but not her struggle for breath.

"You're safe. Breathe."

Her breathing slowed.

"That'a girl. Breathe."

Gradually, her air intake returned to normal.

"You see?" said Tate. "No water. Just sweet, warm air."

She let out a long breath and groaned.

"Oh, Tate. I thought I was —"

"I know. It's a common reaction after a near drowning. I should've been ready for it. My fault."

Caroline relaxed more, her eyelids getting heavier. Tate flicked off the lamp and started for the door.

"Wait," Caroline mumbled, half asleep.

Tate turned around, or rather his silhouette did, backlit by the glow from the doorway.

"Please don't go."

Tate looked in Caroline's direction.

"Stay with me just a little longer."

Tate glanced at the window. Did it seem a bit brighter? He lay down on the bed beside Caroline but on top of the comforter, with a troubled expression. She snuggled against him, putting her head on his right shoulder. She closed her eyes and fell asleep.

Chapter Four

Sunlight on her face awoke her. A single ray streaked the left side of the bed where Tate had lain. Caroline wondered when exactly he'd left her. Throwing off the comforter, she got out of bed and went to the window. The sun shone on the horizon just above the tranquil blue-grey ocean. She moved to the closet, from which she withdrew the pink T-shirt, sweatpants, and ski jacket.

Caroline exited the bedroom carrying the jacket. Tate wasn't on the sofa or anywhere in the den. A glass of orange juice and an apple in a cereal bowl marked her side of the table.

Feeling cold, she noticed the electric fireplace was off. The added chill this gave her had little to do with a lack of heat. Putting on the ski jacket and guzzling the orange juice, she grabbed the apple and hurried to the stairwell, gobbling the fruit on her way down.

She walked out of the lighthouse into a bright yet nippy day. She could see much of the stony island but no sign of its human inhabitant, only a group of seagulls ambling around the pebbled beach by the lighthouse base.

"Tate!" she called out with concern.

A seagull cooed in response, increasing her unease. She began walking toward the south point of the island from where Tate had carried her, unless she'd dreamt that. She recognized the twin grey boulders demarking the cove and soon passed between them. The stretch of beach was just as she recalled it except for one missing element—Tate's sailboat.

She turned to the ocean, desperate to glimpse his golden sail returning. Instead, she spotted a larger, whiter, sleeker boat some fifty yards out, slowly moving left past the island. It had a broad red stripe near the front containing a coat of arms and, within the shield, a vertical American flag.

Caroline ran to the water's edge, frantically waving her arms overhead. After almost a minute, unable to maintain the intense arm motion, she reluctantly let them drop. Seeing the boat slow down, she fell to her knees.

"God bless America," she said.

Minutes later, an orange rubber raft approached her position with two men on board in uniform blue windbreakers, the pilot and an erect young officer. They docked in the same spot Tate's sailboat had. The officer nimbly leapt off the raft and stepped toward Caroline. She saw he wore an incredulous expression under his white Coast Guard officer's cap.

"Caroline York?"

"In the flesh," she said. "Though you look like you're seeing a ghost."

"Forgive me, ma'am. We were out searching for you.... We didn't expect to find you here, like this."

"Alive, you mean."

"Yes, ma…. Sorry. Ensign Tim Bailey, United States Coast Guard, at your service."

"Does that include a lift?"

"Of course."

Ensign Bailey indicated the raft. Caroline started walking toward it at his side.

"I can appreciate your shock, Ensign. I would be out there, frozen stiff, if it hadn't been for the lighthouse keeper."

"Lighthouse keeper, ma'am?"

"Yes — Tate. He plucked me out of the ocean and defrosted me. He said he'd take me to the mainland this morning, but he seems to have left without me."

Ensign Bailey appeared uneasy. They stopped a few feet from the raft. Caroline waved a greeting to the muscular black seaman, who nodded at her.

Ensign Bailey addressed her. "Our medic'll give you a quick checkup to make sure you're okay."

"I'm all right," Caroline said, then noticed the ensign's glum expression. "Or am I?"

"There is no lighthouse keeper, ma'am.

Brighton Lighthouse has been fully automated
for twenty-nine years."

Chapter Five

"So he doesn't work the lighthouse," Caroline said. "But he lives there."

"No, ma'am, nobody does," said Ensign Bailey.

"You must be mistaken. There's furniture up there—a bath, a bed, these clothes."

"Oh. An old couple in New York, the Eckstroms, they sponsor the place. They come up every August and stay a month, leaving some winter articles behind."

"This man was young," said Caroline. "Tall, strong, quite hand…. You don't believe me?"

Ensign Bailey shrugged. "Anything you

say, I'll put in my report. Allow me, ma'am."

He extended a hand to assist Caroline into the launch. She started to take it, then suddenly pulled back.

"Christmas tree!"

"Ma'am?"

"On the mantle—a fresh-cut miniature pine. It couldn't've lasted three weeks, let alone four months."

Ensign Bailey turned to the raft pilot. "We'll be right back, Seaman."

The seaman nodded. As Caroline hurried back toward the lighthouse, Ensign Bailey caught up to her. They stopped before the heavy door, which he pulled open by the brass ring. Caroline steadily climbed the stairwell, with Ensign Bailey close behind. She paused twice to rest before ascending to the den.

Ensign Bailey found her staring at the artificial fireplace, its mantelpiece completely bare. He moved beside her.

"It was right here," she said.

"Yes, ma'am. We'd better go."

Caroline started down the stairwell. She

thought she saw Ensign Bailey cast a worried glance around the den before descending after her. Twelve minutes later, they sat on the raft, skipping toward the Coast Guard cutter. Only Caroline was looking backward at the receding lighthouse.

The cutter sliced through the water at twenty knots, heading north. In the Spartan bridge, Caroline sat in a starboard side chair listening to Ensign Bailey from the command chair. Seaman Wayne Smith, who'd piloted the raft, now steered the larger craft.

"Sorry, we can't contact your folks from here," Ensign Bailey said. "Official com only."

"At least let them know I'm alive," said Caroline.

"You'll be able to call them yourself from the clinic."

"That's another thing. Why can't I go to my doctor in Boston?"

"Regulations. You're still Coast Guard responsibility."

They reached the Portland outskirts just before noon. The cutter approached a remote old wooden pier with an ambulance at the ocean end. Two paramedics, a heavy man and a stout woman, sat in the open back with their feet dangling. Seeing the boat start to dock, they stood up and extracted a stretcher from the ambulance.

"Is that for me?" asked Caroline while being escorted off the portside deck by Ensign Bailey. "I can walk."

Ensign Bailey opened his mouth to say something.

"Don't tell me," said Caroline. "Regulations."

"Yes, ma'am."

The paramedics hoisted Caroline onto the stretcher and into the ambulance, then climbed into the back with her. The woman locked down the stretcher as the man shut the rear doors.

"May I borrow your phone?" Caroline asked the woman.

The ambulance took off with the siren blaring.

"Never mind," Caroline said inaudibly under the siren's wail.

Chapter Six

"You're in good health, Ms. York," Lieutenant William Royce said. "Blood pressure and heart rate show no ill effects from your ordeal."

"Thank goodness," said Caroline.

They stood in a toasty examination room at the East Portland Medical Clinic, Caroline completely redressed, although the physician had just seen her naked. He was a thin, grey-haired, sixty-something man wearing an open medical coat over his Coast Guard officer's uniform.

"However, given all you went through, I

highly recommend a psychological exam."

"I'm all right, Doct— Lieutenant."

"Doc is fine," Royce said amiably. "And you certainly seem to be. But just so you know, I signed Ensign Bailey's report on what probably occurred after you fell off your cruise ship."

"Probably?" Caroline challenged. "I told you exactly what happened, and Ensign Bailey. Did his report say something different?"

"On one point. That you managed to swim into the island's surf zone, where a lucky wave caught you and swept you to shore. In a state of shock, you made it to the lighthouse and did everything right to survive. But the whole time, your mind was playing tricks."

"Like imagining my heroic rescuer?!" Caroline snapped. "Like a silly reader of romance novels?!"

"Are you calling my wife silly?" Doctor Royce said with a feeble smile. "But seriously. Our CO, Commander Talbot, ordered me to sign the report if I found it even remotely plausible following my examination of you. And I must say that I do."

"But he was real — Tate is real."

"Then, you're going to have to produce him because the file on you is officially closed."

Caroline scowled. The door opened, held by a matronly nurse more martial than Royce.

"Doctor, the patient's ride is here. He's waiting in the lobby."

"Thank you, Jill."

Nurse Jill withdrew, closing the door behind her.

"He had to drive up all the way from Boston to free me," Caroline said. "Since you wouldn't release me on my own volition."

"I prefer discharging patients to family members. A fiancé counts. Congratulations on your future wedding to Mr. Fleming."

Caroline looked at Royce. "How'd you know his name?"

"You must've mentioned it."

"I'm sure I didn't."

"Oh, I forgot," Royce said as if recalling something. "It's on the release form you filled out. Merry Christmas, Ms. York."

He left the room rather swiftly for a man his

age. Caroline took her borrowed ski jacket off the stool and exited behind him.

Peter Fleming stood beside the large Christmas tree in the reception area, beaming as Caroline approached him. He threw his arms around her and pressed her to his camel wool coat.

"I thought I'd lost you."

"Me too," said Caroline.

"How do you feel?"

"Shockingly well. I had planned to go into work tomorrow, but Rita forbade it."

"I suppose a near death experience is a viable excuse, even for her," Peter said. "Let's go home, darling."

He put an arm around Caroline's shoulder and escorted her outside.

The silver Jaguar F-Type sped south toward Boston on Interstate 95, its powerful headlights compensating for the sunset gloom. Caroline sat in the plush caramel passenger seat, Peter's cellphone in hand, reading aloud the description below a picture of Brighton Lighthouse.

"Three miles off the coast of southern Maine

lies Brighton Rock with its historic lighthouse, built in seventeen-sixty-one. It once served as a beacon for British troop night landings during the Revolutionary War. Since then, Brighton Lighthouse has ably served its original purpose, and is credited with preventing numerous shipwrecks and saving countless lives."

"Including yours."

"Yes," said Caroline, scrolling down on the screen. "But there's no link to the name 'Tate' and Brighton Lighthouse."

"Maybe you should put him out of your pretty head for a while."

"Why do you say that?"

"May help you remember things a bit more clearly."

Caroline reflected for a moment. "I was in a daze for much of last night, but quite lucid by the end of it, thanks to Tate."

"The Phantom of the lighthouse."

Caroline snapped. "When did you join the Coast Guard?"

"What?"

"They implied the same thing, that Tate

doesn't exist and never did. Tried hard to persuade me of that. Now you're doing it. Almost as if—"

Peter squirmed, and Caroline caught it.

"You talked to him," she said. "Lieutenant Doctor Royce."

"He called me on the drive up. He's concerned you're still traumatized. Thinks I can help you."

"By erasing Tate from my mind."

"He mentioned it."

"That's why he kept me there and had you come get me," Caroline said, partly to herself. "So he could influence you to influence me. But why? What's so provocative about my story? Just because they can't find Tate doesn't mean I made him up."

"Can we forget about the guy for the rest of the drive?"

"All right," said Caroline.

Peter turned to her. "I have an idea. Let's fast forward our Christmas plans. We'll make a quick stop at your place, grab your things, and go to my place—our place once you finally marry me. Carmen'll pamper you the whole time. She likes you more than she likes me, and I pay her."

"Thank you, sweetheart, but I'd like to be alone with my thoughts for a while—and no distractions."

"Like the full court press by me."

"I'm better at foul shots," said Caroline.

Peter tightened his grip on the steering wheel.

Chapter Seven

Christmas lights festooned several windows of the Beacon Street block, although none in Caroline's brownstone row house on the top third floor. Peter stopped his Jaguar by the parked car in front of it and remained sulking behind the wheel.

Caroline leaned into him. "Bear with me, darling. I'm not myself."

Peter looked at her with concern. She pressed her lips to his and gave him a deep, delightful kiss. While he savored it, she got out of the car. Caroline could hear the Jaguar engine idling behind her as she approached her front door and pressed one of the intercom buttons. A male voice answered.

"Yes?"

"Maurice, it's Caroline. Did Ellen leave you a spare key for me?"

"Yeah. So I'll finally get you into my place."

Caroline smiled and said, "I hear enough fashion talk at work. Meet me on the landing."

The front door buzzed. Caroline opened it and turned around to see the Jaguar pull away.

Maurice met her at the top of the third stairway between their two apartments. He was a thin millennial with a mop of red hair and frameless glasses, wearing a blue Boston U sweatshirt and jeans. He fingered a key while appraising Caroline.

"*Sublime* must be in bad shape. That's the dreariest I've ever seen you look."

"It's a long story," said Caroline. "You can read it in the magazine."

"Better have Matthew McConaughey on the cover."

Caroline winked. Maurice smilingly gave her the key.

"Thanks, Maurice."

He went to his apartment on the left. Caroline unlocked the door across from it and entered her small living room. The lit floor lamp in the far right corner illuminated the Persian carpet, brown leather sofa and matching armchair, long granite coffee table, and the twin low bookshelves full of new hardbacks, all given to her by *Sublime* book critic Eric Stevens, who desired her. A wide framed poster of the 2019 Milan Fashion Show covered the right wall, the 2019 Cannes Film Festival, on the left.

She moved right past the modern cupboard containing her fancy china, then left past the two-seat dining table into the narrow kitchen. She came out a minute later with a glass of Bourgogne Pinot Noir and sat down at her desk. On the landline phone, she spoke to her mother in Albany, reassuring her that she was still alive and not yet with her father in Heaven. She normally downplayed her mom's devout Christianity, but tonight she appreciated it, having come so close to the end of her mortal life.

Afterward, she worked on her laptop. The screen displayed a *Portland Press Herald* article and a picture below it. The headline under the photo read MYSTERY MAN SAVES FISHERMAN AND SONS FROM DEATH AT SEA, by Spencer Williams, *Portland Press Herald* Staff Writer. The picture showed a craggy, white-mustached fisherman between a pair of clean-shaven young men standing on a dock. Caroline scrolled down to the story itself.

Joca Mendes was sure the fish off Point Judith would soon have their revenge on him and his two sons when their fishing schooner capsized in the cold ocean just after dark. Until the sudden appearance of a man on a sailboat saved them from that fate.

"He came fast out of nowhere," said Mendes, 48. "Any slower and we wouldn't be here. I know how quick you can die in that water. The man pulled out me and my boys before our time was up."

The stranger dropped Mendes and his sons — Carlos, 21, and Luis, 19 — ashore by the Point Judith Lighthouse, then sailed away. Mendes had activated the distress signal on his capsized vessel, so they knew help was on the way.

"He just took off," Luis said. "Didn't give us his name."

"Or the chance to thank him," said Carlos.

The Mendeses described their rescuer as a well-built man with dark brown hair, in his late twenties or early thirties. They are offering him a reward in public. Below is an artist's sketch of the elusive hero.

Caroline stared at the man in the drawing for a full minute, studying his windswept hair and rugged, handsome face. Of course, she had seen him before.

"Tate," she said aloud.

Chapter Eight

Caroline exited the Downtown Crossing subway station in a gold wool long coat with a wraparound belt that defied the murky late morning. Outside the station gate, she heard and saw an old black street saxophonist masterfully blowing out *God Rest Ye, Merry Gentlemen*. She started to bypass him, but the song made her stop. She listened to the entire piece, recalling when she'd heard it last, in the lighthouse with Tate. She opened her faux alligator purse and dropped a ten-dollar bill in the open sax case. The musician looked up at her.

"Thank you, miss," he said in a gravelly

voice.

"Sounded lovely."

"You got more out of it than other folks."

The old man indicated his instrument case, empty except for her contribution.

"It reminded me of someone."

"Someone special to you?"

"Yes," said Caroline, surprising herself.

The man raised the saxophone to his lips and began blowing out *It Came upon a Midnight Clear*. Caroline swallowed. Coincidence, she thought—just another famous Christmas carol. She walked away, heading west on Franklin Street. Two blocks down, she entered the Taylor Office Building, a venerable grey dwarf amid modern skyscrapers.

~*~

The *Sublime Magazine* offices comprised most of the top fifth floor, with Rita Lyton's corner office the size of three others. Rita sat behind her antique mahogany desk, a red felt pen in hand, marking up a six-page Word printout. Paul Scott calmly watched her edit in the leather guest chair farther from the door. Rita lowered the document and blew air through her closed lips.

"I know Karen is nowhere near the writer Caroline is," she said. "But this is Cliche Central."

"You should've read it before I got to it," said Paul.

"I can imagine." Rita read aloud, "'As a freshman in Congress, Christina Hartley plans to take on the system.' Yawn."

"Yeah, every politician plans to take on the system—till the money starts pouring in."

"The only reason we're featuring Hartley is because she's sexy," said Rita. "Here."

She plopped down the document pages on Paul's side of the desktop.

"Tell Karen to cut out the feminist BS and focus on what's unique about Congresswoman Hartley—her social life. And she'll have to name her rocker boyfriend."

"Right," said Paul, standing up. He picked up the document just as the door opened. Paul grinned. "Caroline!"

Rita also smiled, but only for a second, as

Paul embraced Caroline.

"I'm sorry," he said. "Took me way too long to realize you'd fallen off the boat."

"No one's fault, Paul."

"By the time we circled back, you were gone."

"But not forgotten," said Rita. "I gave you the week off, Caroline. That's a rare indulgence for me."

Caroline broke off the hug with Paul and turned to Rita. "I need ten minutes of your time."

Paul held up the document. "I got work to do," he said, then aside to Caroline, continued. "What're you doing, Christmas Eve?"

"I'm supposed to attend an all-day banquet with Peter's firm, but I may have other plans," said Caroline, then raising her voice said, "Depending on our fabulous boss."

Rita smiled.

"Dinner, our house," said Paul.

"Next week."

Paul patted Caroline's shoulder with the printout and left the office. She turned to Rita.

"I'm very happy to see you, Caroline."

"Thanks, Rita. It was surreal, literally. That's what I came to talk to you about."

"Have a seat."

Caroline sat down in the closer visitor's chair. Rita pushed a button on her desk phone. "Julie, hold my calls for ten minutes."

"Yes, Ms. Lyton," said Julie's voice.

Rita looked expectantly at Caroline.

"I know Peter told you what happened to me," said Caroline. "After my involuntary swim."

"He knew how upset we all were and called with the welcome news of your rescue."

"Did he mention my rescuer?"

"The lighthouse keeper who wasn't."

"He's something, Rita, and somewhere. He saved at least three other people before me and left them for the Coast Guard to pick up, like he did me, only at another lighthouse location."

"Maybe he's a lighthouse fetishist and ashamed of it."

"Or a fugitive from justice," said Caroline. "I suspect the Coast Guard knows more about him than they're letting on. In fact, they are deliberately obscuring him."

"You're not suggesting a government conspiracy?"

Caroline shrugged. "Could make a great story."

"Sure, for the *Boston Globe*. And you're no longer a reporter there. You're *Sublime Magazine* now. You know, the silly women's beat that pays our rent—gossip, glamour, romance, fashion."

"Romance," said Caroline.

She drew a folded sheet of paper from her purse, leaned over Rita's desk, and passed it to her. Rita unfolded the paper and looked at it.

"What is this, a new Marvel superhero?"

"It's an artist's sketch of Tate, provided by the men he rescued two years ago."

Rita studied the paper with a glimmer of interest. "Hmm. He might appeal to some women. Those naively longing for a knight in shining arm—" She cleared her throat, interrupting herself. "What have you got in mind?"

"Give me two weeks to track him down," said Caroline. "If I can't find him by then, I'll write my thrilling survival at sea story. It's a win-win for the mag."

Rita glanced at the paper in her hand. "You have one week. Deadline New Year's Eve. I'll, ah, just keep this for my files."

She refolded the paper and placed it in the top right desk drawer.

Chapter Nine

Caroline drove her maroon 2019 Ford Escape SUV east on Route 128 in an early evening drizzle, its wiper blades accompanying *The Nutcracker Suite* on the stereo. Passing through Gloucester at dusk, she appreciated the town's vintage postcard look, now more Christmas card-like, given the pervasive decorations. At the last exit before the ocean, she turned off on a beachside road. The grey waves lapping at her driver's window, discomforted her. This was the closest she'd come to the ocean since it almost killed her, and she had the grim feeling it wanted another crack at her.

Soon she got even closer to the water on a peninsular strip bearing a single white wood, two-story cottage. She turned into its gravel driveway and stopped beside a black mailbox with a painted seagull on the side. Peering out the window through the rain and gloom, she visually confirmed the sea bird, depicted in mid-dive. She continued to the cottage and parked next to the only other vehicle in front of it, a green pickup truck.

She dashed to the roofed porch carrying a fancy liquor gift bag. Before stepping on the doormat, she read the words on it. Home is the sailor, home from sea, And the hunter home from the hill. She remembered the line from her Wellesley English Lit major days, though not the precise source. She pressed the doorbell, triggering a chime rendition of *Blow the Man Down*. On the last chime, Captain Fowler opened the door wearing a green knit sweater and a smile.

"Ahoy, mermaid."

"Some mermaid," Caroline said. "I nearly drowned."

"You came through, thank God."

"And man. One man in particular. He's the reason I'm here."

Captain Fowler quit smiling and opened the door wider. "Come in."

Caroline entered a warm living room marked by tasteful Americana furniture, other than an antique sea chest serving as the coffee table. The nautical flavor continued on the back wall, where hung three paintings of classic schooners plus one notable exception — a black-and-white photo of a PT boat on a jungle river with three young navy men on deck. The crackling fireplace, twinkling Christmas tree, and country Christmas music added seasonal warmth. As the door shut behind her, she noticed a full duffel bag just to the right of it.

"Nice place, Captain."

"Thank you. My wife made it cozy for when I came in from the sea."

"Well, you're not at sea now, or I under it."

Caroline handed Captain Fowler the gift bag. He pulled out an ornate squat bottle of rum. His smile returned.

"Facundo Paraiso, Bacardi. You know, I used to run guns to Cuba for the Bacardi family, right under Castro's nose. Didn't do any good, but we still got the best of it, like this stuff. Let's drink to that. Please."

He indicated the blue armchair near the fireplace, and Caroline sat down in it. She watched her host approach a Dutch mahogany cabinet. He extended two rods from the midsection and lowered a previously hidden flap onto them, revealing a well-stocked bar. He put the rum bottle on the flap and withdrew two glasses. Caroline turned back to the living room, again noting the full duffel bag by the door.

"Going somewhere, Captain?"

Captain Fowler began opening the rum bottle. "Greece. Sailing Christmas Day. I'll be spending all next year retracing Homer's Odyssey for Harvard kids."

"That's fantastic. Guess I caught you just in time."

Captain Fowler poured the rum in the two glasses, frowning slightly. Not from the effort, thought Caroline.

"About the Coast Guard account of your survival. You may wanna go with it."

"What?!" balked Caroline. "That a lucky wave scooped me up and deposited me ashore? I know you don't believe that."

Captain Fowler approached her with a full glass in each hand. She stared at him.

"You said you had information on Tate you couldn't tell me on the phone."

"I'm loath to tell you now," said Captain Fowler. "For your sake."

"My sake?"

"Yes, missy. You crossed a barrier reef that night—from the known to the unknown and back again. Dwelling on the far shoal might disturb you."

"I'm already disturbed," said Caroline. "As in questioning my sanity."

"My tale will make you doubt it, and mine." Captain Fowler handed Caroline her glass of rum.

"Please, Captain. I have to know."

"Very well. I was saving the story for my

book, but you're part of it now. Drink up. You'll want to be high for this."

Caroline sipped the rum, savoring its strong, sweet taste. Captain Fowler moved to the fireplace. He took a long swig of his rum and placed the glass on the mantelpiece. He grabbed the poker and began stoking the flame.

"Does it feel odd to you — to be alive?"

"Yes," Caroline said without hesitation. "Even two days later."

Captain Fowler nodded. "You had no earthly chance of surviving your peril — only an unearthly one. Blessedly for you, it's Christmastime, when Heaven and Earth are at their closest, and miracles abound. Your miracle began long before you hit the water — about five years ago, in Marsport."

Riveted, Caroline hit the record function on her cellphone and laid it on the armrest. "There's a small Coast Guard station there, normally four Guardsmen per shift. It being Christmas Eve night, there were only two...."

A Christmas Ghost Story

The Marsport Coast Guard substation is a single-story facility three miles north of Marsport via the winding cliffside road, or two straight miles by sea. From its short pier, on a clear night, you can see the town lights across the bay. But that blizzardy Christmas Eve, there was not a flicker. Two snow-dusted vessels were tied to the pier—a small rescue boat and a smaller speedboat.

The interior was a single office with five metal desks—two sets of two pressed against each other, and the dispatcher's desk facing the right window and pier. The commander's pine desk dominated the left side. Only the first set of desks was occupied. In the left desk sat stocky brown Ensign Gustavo Perez reading a Dean Koontz paperback novel. Across from him, Ensign Jack Tate glanced at the analog wall clock for the second time that minute—eight-forty-four.

"Clockwatcher," said Perez, looking up from his book.

"The time has come," Tate said.

He opened his top desk drawer and took

out a gold cigar tube. He tossed the tube to Perez, who caught it. Perez twisted the tube open and withdrew a healthy dark cigar.

"Whoa," he said, fingering the cigar. "We're supposed to intercept these from coming into our country. Thank you, Jack."

"It's not a gift, Gus. It's a bribe."

"What I gotta do for it? I'm only a poor corrupt official."

"Let me split two hours early, without Talbot finding out. Guy's a walking rulebook."

"Don't tell me," Perez said. "You got a girl waiting."

"Not just any girl, amigo, the next Miss Maine."

"That's how you described your last one — Judy."

"Julie. She failed the talent competition. Donna has a better shot."

"Not with you, long term."

"Hey, I'll get hitched," said Tate. "One of these days."

"You'll find it a lot more rewarding than playing the field — and more relaxing."

"That's easy for you to say. You married Susan."

Perez grinned. "And turned her into a double mom. And she still loves me.

"You're a lucky guy."

"No kidding. You may think you're flying high with a different chick of the month, but you're really wasting precious time and Christmas magic. You know what Suzy and I will be doing dawn tomorrow? Sitting by the tree before the kids wake up, just to see the looks on their faces as they unwrap their presents. That's what it's all about, Jack."

"Does sound nice," said Tate. "I'll just have to suffer a while longer—with your help."

Perez sighed. "What if a call comes in? It's getting pretty rough out there."

"You give me a ring. I'll be at the Emerald Isle till midnight, just ten minutes away."

"Keep your phone on, even in mid-makeout."

Tate smiled. "Thanks, Gus. Merry Christmas."

He stood up and dashed to the front door,

plucked his ensign's cap and uniform coat off the coat rack, and put them on and left.

Tate drove his blue Chevrolet Spark south on Lookout Road, the wipers brushing off snowflakes to Dean Martin's *Let it Snow*. There was no other traffic in either lane two hours before Christmas Day. He kept to the forty-mile-per hour-speed limit. Usually, he went well over it despite the twisting road's close proximity to the cliff edge and the sixty-foot ocean drop beyond, but he knew an ice patch could be fatal. A mile from Marsport, he felt one — in his spine. He shuddered but put it out of his mind.

He came down the steep hill into Marsport at sea level. Passing Main Street, he drove into the Emerald Isle lot, across the street from the ocean. Three cars occupied the parking strip in front, with room for twelve. His Spark made four. He approached the small green awning and went inside.

The place seemed cozier than usual, possibly due to the holly wreaths lining the pinewood bar, the Irish Christmas music on the sound system, and the few customers. An old man sat alone at the bar sipping a Guinness. The bartender, a red-faced, fiftyish man with crewcut white hair, waved at Tate.

"Hey, Pat," Tate said.

"Of course. Pretty lass comes in all alone on the night before Christmas. I should've figured you'd be turnin' up."

Tate smiled and went into the booth area. He passed a booth with two somber men drinking whisky to approach the last booth on the left. A striking twenty-something brunette sat nursing a fizzy soda while flattering a pink velvet sweater. Donna smiled at Tate and slid further into the booth. He sat down beside her and pecked her on the lips, then nodded at her drink.

"Ginger ale?"

"I never drink alone," said Donna.

"I doubt you ever have to."

"Not even ten minutes ago."

Tate glanced at the booth with the two men. The one facing them averted his eyes.

"I believe your dry spell's over," said Tate,

waving his hand.

"Okay."

"Irish coffee?"

"Sounds good."

A cute blonde waitress with a pug nose approached them.

"Two Irish coffees, Rowena," Tate said. "Hers with cream on top."

"How sweet," said Donna.

Three rounds later, only two for Donna, they sat pressed against each other in intimate conversation, Tate talking.

"So I thought, why join the navy to do my patriotic duty? Spend three months a stretch aboard some giant ship, among a bunch of surly men, when I could be serving Uncle Sam right here on shore, enjoying the company of a gorgeous babe."

"Aww. And far away from war."

"Well, I still expect to see some action."

"Really? Where?"

"Your place or mine," said Tate.

Donna smiled coyly. "You just might, sailor."

They kissed a second time, this time intensely.

Behind the bar, Patrick answered the ringing landline phone. He had to speak loudly over the Irish music and strained to hear the voice on the line.

"Emerald Isle...Hey, Gustavo.... Yeah, he's here, scoring with another hot—" Pat tensed while listening to the caller talk. "Oh my. I'll go tell 'im. Be safe out there, man."

Tate looked up from a deep kiss with Donna to see Pat standing right beside the booth. "What's up, Pat?"

"Perez has been calling you for fifteen minutes with an SOS."

Tate snatched his cellphone off the seat cushion and looked at the screen. The muted symbol showed clearly along with six calls from "Station."

"Oh no," Tate said, then turned to the upset Donna. "I gotta go, babe. I'll call you."

He stood up, put on his uniform coat, and sprinted out the front door. Under the awning, with the music fainter, he put his cellphone to his ear. He grew more anxious with each ring until he got an answer.

"Gus!" he said, then listened. "How far out? … Wait for me. I'm on my way! Don't take off without me!"

Tate ran to his car and jumped in. He screeched out of the parking strip and turned left, going north on Lookout Road in the direction he'd come from.

The Spark climbed the hill with wipers on full blast. Tate took the highland curves at sixty-miles-per hour, the cliff edge on his right a constant hazard. Beginning the mile-long descent to the Coast Guard station, he put his foot on the brake. The car sped up, front tires sliding on an ice patch. Where the road wound left, the Spark went straight, heading toward the low guardrail that demarked the cliff edge. Tate turned the steering wheel left with all his might, to no avail.

A few yards from the guardrail, the car spun left. It shot across both lanes into a pine tree patch and crashed against the nearest trunk. The front hood crumpled, and the airbag deployed, trapping Tate behind the wheel. Half conscious, he lost all sense of time.

At some point, the urgency of his mission came back to him. Tate tried to squeeze out from behind the airbag only to realize he had to first unbuckle his seatbelt. With much fumbling, he did. He wiggled left against the airbag, making slow, awkward progress, but finally managed to reach the driver's door and open it. He dropped out on the soft snow as more snow fell on him.

Unsteadily, he rose to his feet, brushing snowflakes off his forehead — he had left his cap in the bar, along with Donna. But the only person on his mind just then was Gus, who must have cast off on the rescue boat without him. Tate had one chance to catch up to Gus — the speedboat, if he could get to the station in time. He looked at his smashed Spark. It wasn't going anywhere.

Knowing he had to call the Marsport Police and have them rush him to the station, he reached into one coat pocket for his cellphone, then the other. It wasn't in either. He turned to the car, the driver's door still open, and could see nothing inside but the bloated airbag. His phone had to be stuck under it. He wanted to scream.

Tate looked down the road, what he could see of it in the dark and snow. It was less than a mile to the station, all downhill—he could get there in twenty minutes on foot, less if he caught a ride. He crossed the road to the ocean side, ready to start his jog when a light beam from the sea caught his eye. Approaching the guardrail with foreboding, Tate stared out over the water far below. He identified the beam, about a mile out and distancing. It was the searchlight on a Coast Guard rescue boat, specifically the one from Marsport Station, its red lights flashing on top of the pilothouse.

Tate ran across the road to his Spark and yanked open the passenger door, and noticed the glove compartment was clear of the airbag. Pulling down the latch, he took out a pair of magnification eight naval binoculars and a flashlight, then ran back to the cliff edge and looked through the binoculars at the Coast

Guard boat.

The searchlight illuminated a half capsized old fishing trawler facing land. It was tilted portside, about to overturn, with four men lying prostrate on the deck while grasping to it for dear life. The inclined top-heavy masthead appeared to be accelerating the vessel's finish.

The rescue boat approached the trawler on its sunken side and stopped very close to it. The men clinging to the boat appeared more than ready to swim to the other one.

"Good job, Gus," said Tate.

Gus emerged from the pilothouse to the prow deck in his uniform coat. He went straight to the anchor line and pulled the release lever. The weighty Knox anchor sank between the boats. Tate kept the binoculars fixed on his partner.

Gus pulled a compressed rope ladder from the deck compartment. He clasped the two hooks to the handrail and threw down the rope. He yelled something to the men on the trawler.

"One at a time," Tate assumed.

The leftmost man released his grip and

slid into the water. He swam to the rescue boat and grabbed a low rung of the rope ladder. Behind him, the trawler twisted again, forcing the other three men to tighten their handholds. The masthead leaned closer to the Coast Guard boat.

"Gus, get out of there," Tate said nervously.

The man on the rope ladder started to climb it. Gus bent over the handrail to help him. Suddenly, both men stopped. They turned their faces to the trawler masthead just in time to see it hurtling down toward them. It was the last thing they ever saw. The masthead hammered the Coast Guard boat and broke. The trawler flipped upside down, thrusting the three men on it underwater. Tate could almost hear their muffled screams.

"No!" he cried.

He stared at the twin wrecks, knowing Gus was dead and the others too. Eerily, the rescue boat's searchlight remained lit, shining on the snowy, empty sea. He lowered the binoculars, his tears mixing with snowflakes. He turned to the road and froze.

A man stood facing him, wearing a hooded crimson cloak that came down to below the knees, slightly open in front, the lace at his throat. The slight part revealed what resembled a purple catsuit, only thicker at the boots and split by a gold belt. The hood hid his face but not the Van Dyke beard. Tate addressed the stranger.

"Hey, man, where's your car? I'm a Coast Guard officer. Need to get to the station down the road."

The man said nothing and appeared to be staring at Tate. Tate bristled.

"My partner is dead! And four other men. I gotta report it."

"They shall accost you," the stranger said in what sounded like a British accent.

"What?"

"You left your post," the man said, his classic English accent clearer. "Allowed your comrade-in-arms to perish, along with the rest. Your life is ruined."

Tate felt another ice patch on his spine, even colder than the one in the car. The man couldn't possibly know what he seemed to know. Only impossibly? Tate dismissed the mad thought. "Who are you?"

"Gareth of Orkney," the man said. "Though, alas, Orkney no longer exists."

He moved past Tate's left shoulder. Tate turned with him, keeping him in sight. He stopped on the edge of the cliff, looking outward. Tate followed his gaze to the disaster at sea.

"You should be on that vessel," said Gareth.

"Don't you think I know that?!"

The shock hit Tate the moment he spoke. Gareth had voiced his despair. He didn't want to know how.

"You chose desire over duty," said Gareth. "An infamy on any night. Only 'tis Christmas Eve, a sacred time for kin. Yet tonight, five husbands are drowned, five women widowed, twelve children deprived of fathers."

"I know two of them. And their mom, Susan."

"For them, Christmas shall evermore bring sorrow rather than joy."

"For me, too," said Tate. "You called it, mister. I'll be spending all my Christmases in prison from now on. Lieutenant Talbot will see to that."

"There is a higher authority than your commander. And He offers you a different form of atonement."

"How do I atone for that?" Tate said, gazing at the lighted wreck.

"As a man, only by confinement, of no value to others. But as a visitant, you can ride the waves at Yuletide, saving folks from harm."

"A visitant...?"

"Neither flesh nor spirit, something betwixt the two."

A mighty wave crashed against the rocks far below.

"You're crazy."

Gareth sighed, then took a step forward, right off the edge of the cliff.

"What?!" gasped Tate.

He rushed to the precipice's edge. Peering down into the darkness, he plucked the flashlight from his coat pocket and shone it on the crashing waves below, in search of a battered corpse.

"Shall I continue?" Gareth said in his left ear.

Tate jumped in his skin and spun to the voice. Gareth stood beside him, looking whole.

"You seem to be doing that," said Tate.

"I have learned to spare superfluous talk o'er a thousand years."

"A thou—"

A siren interrupted Tate, distant but nearing fast. He focused on Gareth.

"Why me? Why do I get this break?"

"You are skilled at seacraft and salvation," said Gareth. "You can be a fisher of men."

"So Christmastime, I'm running around saving people. Where am I the rest of the year?"

"Elsewhere in a half-mortal state."

"For how long? A thousand years like you?"

The siren sounded louder, close now and clearly police. It was coming from the north, the Coast Guard station side. Tate knew they were coming for him.

"Five," said Gareth. "One for each man

who perished this night."

"And after that?"

"You succeed me as a Christmas spirit for a millennium. Unless...." Gareth hesitated.

"Unless?"

"There is a third destiny, albeit most improbable. 'Tis a plea by your departed comrade."

Gareth nodded toward the ocean. Tate shuddered.

"Gus? He's still...around?"

"Indeed. And he hath forgiven you."

"I wish I could," Tate said.

"He begs a boon on your behalf, which my Lord shall ponder during your time of trial."

"What boon?"

Garth started to reply. Tate strained to hear him over the now screaming siren.

"Choose," Gareth concluded. "'Tis now or never."

"How?"

Gareth extended a palm to the cliff edge. "The olden way. A leap of faith."

The screech of tires behind them ended the

siren's wail. Tate turned around to see a white Chevy Tahoe SUV beside his car, roof lights flashing, a gold shield on the door.

"Coast guard police," said Tate, glancing to his right — where Gareth no longer was.

Two large military policemen in navy blue uniform coats and caps stepped out of the SUV, a fortyish veteran holding a cellphone, and his rookie partner brandishing a SIG Sauer service pistol. They warily crossed the road toward Tate, Rookie with a lowered weapon, Veteran with a phone to ear. They halted just short of the guardrail.

"Ensign Tate?" said Veteran. "Lieutenant Talbot wants to see you."

"I bet he does," said Tate.

"Come with us."

"Tell Talbot I'm sorry," Tate said. "I disgraced our uniform."

He turned and sprang off the cliff. Both MPs vaulted over the guardrail and gazed down at the turbulent surf. After a while, Rookie holstered his pistol.

Chapter Ten

Caroline gulped an extra large portion of rum.

"Are you telling me Tate is dead?

Captain Fowler stoked the fireplace for the sixth time since he began his narrative. "Hard to say. But if the yarn is true, he's not exactly alive."

"That's impossible."

"Yes," said Captain Fowler, gazing at the flame. "So was getting pulled out of the North Sea by a mate I'd last seen sinking 'neath the Indian Ocean. That tale will be in my book."

"Who's your source on this one?"

"An old Coast Guard dog, after plenty of these." Captain Fowler raised his rum glass and drank from it.

"Wait," said Caroline. "If the Coast Guard knows about Tate, why are they pressuring me to deny him?"

"I can think of one reason—Phil Talbot. He's a big shot commander now, hoping to make admiral. And he'll bode no scuttlebutt about a disgraced, deceased officer haunting his command. Too embarrassing. He's erased all mention of Jack Tate, even his obituary."

"No wonder I couldn't find any links to him," Caroline said.

Captain Fowler nodded.

"You know," said Caroline. "Talbot's isn't the only career this story can ruin. Mine too as a serious journalist, if I try to peddle a ghost story. My editor might fire me and never print it. I wouldn't blame her. I should scoff at it myself. Yet it all seems so eerily consistent."

"You sensed something different about Tate, but your mind couldn't accept it."

"He was—extraordinary." Caroline shut

off her cellphone's record function.

"So you're scrubbing it?" asked Captain Fowler.

"Not if I can find a firsthand witness."

"Too bad, there's only one, and he's...." Captain Fowler went quiet while looking at Caroline. "Now, wait just a minute."

"Tate," said Caroline.

"You're off your head."

"He rescued me once. He might again. It's still Yuletide, isn't it? Two days before Christmas."

"You're dealing with supernatural forces. They may be less friendly next time round."

"The people have a right to know," said Caroline. "I have to know."

Captain Fowler looked intently at her. "For a more personal reason than your story. Am I right?"

"Perhaps."

"That fiancé of yours will blow his top. Back on the boat, he kept threatening to sue me even while I searched for you."

"I'm sorry to hear it. You'd already saved

my life by forcing me to wear that vest. Please, Captain, will you help me once more?"

"Aye," said Captain Fowler.

Chapter Eleven

The Zenith Tower was a twenty-three-story, narrow-sided, blue glass condo building in Fenway, each floor a single apartment. Shortly after six in the evening, a black limousine pulled into the floodlit driveway and stopped beside the entrance. The Filipino chauffeur opened his door, preparing to exit the vehicle.

"It's all right, Ramon," said Caroline in the back seat, her hand on the right door handle. "But Mr. Fleming—"

"Will never know."

Ramon closed the driver's door as Caroline got out of the limo. She wore a clinging knee-length black cocktail dress with white speckles, long sleeves, and a low round top and carried her grey faux fur jacket on her arm. The building's double doors parted before her.

In the marble lobby, she walked past the Christmas-decorated sitting area to the elevator doors ahead. Behind the security desk, a cute collegian in the uniform blue jacket greeted her.

"Good evening, Miss York."

"Hey, Jeff. Having a nice Christmas?"

"Thanks to residents like Mr. Fleming."

"Hope you got his present early," Caroline muttered to herself while smiling at Jeff.

She pressed the nineteenth floor button in the elevator. It opened on a short corridor that went left to an ornate door and right to a plain one. She went left. The lock clicked as she reached the door, which she effortlessly pushed inward.

She entered a vast apartment with an open living room, bar, and dining area, and a wide rear window view of the Charles River at night. The living room had tasteful Scandinavian furniture on a square white carpet that left a wood-floor path between it and the cedar bar on the right. This led to the antique dining table by the window, with six high-backed white chairs. Only the left head of the table and the place beside it on the far side were set for dinner.

Caroline hung her coat in the foyer closet, taking a perfume gift box out of one pocket. Twenty feet to the right of the table, the kitchen door swung outward. A short Latina Indian maid wearing a grey uniform and her dark hair in a bun emerged with two water goblets. Seeing Caroline approach, she beamed.

"*Dona* Carolina."

"*Hola*, Carmen," Caroline said, smiling.

Carmen put both goblets on the table and stared. Caroline handed her the present.

"*Feliz Navidad.*"

"*Gracias*," said Carmen. "But seeing you alive is the best gift. We had a bad night, Don Peter and I. We thought you were—"

"I know."

"Don Peter is on the phone in the study. He said, please start without him, and he will join you soon."

Caroline sat down in the set place with her back to the window, a small bowl of salad in front of her. Carmen started filling her wineglass with a bottle of Roja Gran Reserva Spanish red.

"Hey, Carmen?"

"Si, Senora?"

"I wish you to know—if things become *dificil* between Don Peter and me, please stay in touch with me."

"I understand," said Carmen. "Thank you."

Peter appeared in the den, still wearing his blue-grey power suit with a gold tie. He went around the head of the table to Caroline's chair as Carmen disappeared into the kitchen.

"Hello, darling," said Peter.

He bent down to Caroline's upturned face and gave her a kiss on the lips. She automatically returned it. Peter sat down and raised his wineglass to her. "To Mr. and Mrs. Peter Fleming—one of these nights."

Caroline clinked glasses with him, and they both took a sip of wine.

"You look stunning, as always," said Peter.

"You're sweet."

"No, proud. Knowing how much you'll raise my status at the club tomorrow while giving the new attorneys something to envy apart from my partnership."

Caroline forced a smile and stuck a fork in her arugula. Peter started on his.

"Just wish *our* partnership was a done deal," said Peter. "Fitzpatrick keeps nagging me about that. He's old school Boston. Likes to think of the firm as family, and you as his future daughter-in-law."

"Almost his late daughter-in-law."

Peter cringed. "I didn't bring that up at work."

"What, that you were nearly single again? Seems it would make prime office gossip, especially among the girls."

"That's not funny, Caroline."

"Seriously, then, why the blackout?"

"So you won't have to answer stupid questions the whole banquet."

"And describe my *incredible* rescue."

"We agreed to let some time go by before discussing it."

"Him, you mean."

Peter swallowed an indelicate amount of wine. "Yeah."

"No worries, sweetheart," said Caroline. "I can't make the banquet tomorrow."

"What?!"

"I'll be working on a story, all day and night."

Peter plopped down his wineglass, spilling a little red on the table mat. "What story?"

"You don't want to know."

"Tate," Peter said through gritted teeth.

"I may have a lead on him. I've got to follow it."

"That's unacceptable."

"Certainly inconvenient," Caroline said, empathically adding, "I'm sorry."

"I've been very patient with you, Caroline."

"Above and beyond the rules of engagement."

"You agreed to marry me, and I to wait till you were ready. I knew you had a lot to sort out. But since your ordeal the other night, you've become increasingly distant. And now you're going to make me look bad with my peers."

"Not my intention."

"Tell me the truth."

"That I promise," said Caroline.

"Is there another man?"

Caroline reflected for a moment. Peter unintentionally held his breath.

"No, Peter. There's no other *man*."

Peter exhaled. "Then come to the banquet tomorrow."

"I can't."

"Damn it, Caroline, I'm through being a pushover. I'm setting our wedding date right now — the first Saturday in April. I'll take either your 'yes' or my ring back by Christmas Day, the day after tomorrow."

"That's fair enough," said Caroline, placing her fork in the salad bowl. "I'd better go."

She rose to her feet. Moving behind Peter, she brushed the back of his neck then continued to the front door.

~*~

Carmen came out of the kitchen with two plates full of golden trout and brown rice and noticed Caroline by the foyer closet extracting her faux fur coat. Carmen placed one dinner plate in front of Peter and held on to the second. By the time she turned around, Caroline was gone.

Peter took out his cellphone and tapped several keys. The other line rang loudly in speaker mode, followed by a man's deep voice.

"Lomax Detective Agency."

"Got a job for you, Frank," said Peter.

"Holiday rate."

"Agreed."

"I'm listening."

"It's a tail job," said Peter.

"Target?"

Peter winced. "Caroline York. Thirty-twenty-nine Beacon Road."

"Check."

The line clicked dead. Peter put down his phone, picked up the knife and fork, and began slicing the trout with unnecessary force.

Chapter Twelve

The old woman walking her Yorkie west on Beacon Street at dawn took no notice of the black Buick Sedan parked several cars from Caroline's rowhouse, despite the steam coming out the tailpipe and the country song coming through the passenger window. The man behind the wheel watched her go by while sipping from a coffee thermos cap. Frank Lomax looked quite fit for someone over fifty, as his tight black sweatshirt, blue jeans, and white running shoes exhibited, although multiple wrinkles and thin grey hair betrayed his age. A brown sheepskin coat lay on the passenger seat. Feeling warm enough without it, he turned off the ignition.

He had just restarted the motor when Caroline York came out of the house, wearing a light blue ski suit and carrying a Barnes & Noble tote bag. She turned right on the sidewalk, away from Lomax. She walked past two cars, then to the street side of her Ford Escape.

As Caroline pulled out of the car line, Lomax got ready to do likewise but hesitated when she made a U-turn and drove by his Buick. He began to follow her at the standard undetectable distance of two cars behind, an easy job in the morning rush-hour traffic.

She turned left on Brookline Avenue, as did Lomax. Both vehicles got on the Massachusetts Turnpike eastbound, then the US-1 north. It was a gray yet bright morning, with the hidden sun radiating the cloud cover. They maintained a steady seventy-five-mile-per-hour pace for over an hour, passing the Welcome to New Hampshire sign just after ten. Forty-two minutes later, they were on Memorial Bridge going over the Piscataqua River into Maine.

The Escape went past a small green sign

and slowed. Lomax looked at the sign while reducing his own speed. It read Kittery — Next Exit. The Escape took the next off-ramp, as did the Buick. In a right-turn lane, Lomax had no option but to get directly behind Caroline's car. It veered onto a two-lane road approaching the Atlantic Ocean. Lomax let a meat truck go by before following it and Caroline.

The road turned into Kittery's Main Street, colonial-style shops on both sides resplendent with Christmas lights and bustling with late customers. Caroline drove past the business district to the marina at the end of the street. A row of boats with and without masts faced the ocean. Most appeared vacant, as did the parking spaces in front of them. Caroline took a spot near the only store building around, Yancy's Marine Supplies and Boat Charters. An Open sign hung on the door below a Christmas wreath.

Caroline started walking right alongside the row of boats, checking the names on the back of each non-sailboat. She failed to see Lomax park on the opposite side of her SUV. He got out of the car, now in his sheepskin coat, and began following her on foot. To the unsuspicious, like Caroline, he was just another wannabe boater admiring the local sea crafts.

~*~

Caroline passed a sleek aluminum boat with the word Mako in bold letters. Six vessels farther, she stopped behind an old but well-preserved yacht, the Aegir. It was about eight-hundred feet long with a blue hull, white deck, and orange pilothouse. Choral Christmas music played somewhere inside. Captain Fowler emerged from the pilothouse lugging a can of white paint. Spotting Caroline on the dock, he smiled.

"Ahoy, mermaid."

"What or who is Aegir?" Caroline asked.

"The Norse god of the sea."

"But you're a Christian."

"Out there, I'd welcome any backup," Captain Fowler said, nodding seaward.

Caroline glimpsed a solid middle-aged man in a sheepskin coat, inspecting the sailboat two slots to her left. He seemed more cowboy than sailor. She mentally dismissed him and turned back to the Aegir.

"You ready to ship out?" Captain Fowler asked.

"Aye aye, Skipper. Request permission to come aboard."

"Granted, missy."

Captain Fowler held out a hand and helped Caroline climb onto the stern deck.

~*~

Lomax started inauspiciously walking back the way he had come. Five boats away from the Aegir, he broke into a run. He reached the boat supplies store, swung open the door, and darted inside.

It was a hardware-like store with orderly rows of marine gear. A loaded speargun hung on the back wall. The only occupant sat behind the counter—an overweight fortyish man with long dark hair in a red flannel shirt reading a *Game of Thrones* paperback. He peered over his book at the clearly impatient visitor.

"Your sign says you charter boats," said Lomax.

"Not on Christmas Eve. 'Fraid you're out of luck."

"How much to change my luck fast?"

The shopkeeper studied Lomax. "A thousand bucks just to cast off."

Lomax took out his cellphone, hit a few keys, and listened to the ring on the other line.

~*~

Peter's cellphone rang on the mahogany desk in his corner office at the law firm of Fitzpatrick, Stewart, and Fleming. Conversing on the landline phone, Peter glanced at the mobile's caller ID and stiffened.

"Gotta take this, Brian," he said. "See you at the banquet." He hung up the desk phone and picked up the mobile. "Where are you now?... Kittery—Maine...Who's the owner?.... Fowler!.... Spend what you need. I'll cover it.... Call me back."

Peter put down the cellphone with a grimace.

Chapter Thirteen

The Aegir sailed north at twenty knots, keeping two miles east of the Maine coastline. Captain Fowler sat in the white mariner's chair on the minimalist bridge, steering the boat, Caroline in the right seat, nibbling a tuna sandwich. The windows offered good visibility in four directions. At half past three, the sun was already sinking overland.

"Second thoughts?" Captain Fowler asked.

"More like fifth ones."

"What's your latest?"

"Stop this lunacy, go back to Boston."

"Say the word, and I'll turn the boat

around."

"It's tempting, but no," said Caroline. "I feel I'm getting close to something extraordinary."

"And someone."

"That is the question, isn't it—who or what is Tate?"

"Which would you rather he be?"

"I don't know," said Caroline. "Yet." She finished the sandwich and took a long drink of bottled water.

"I suppose there's magic either way," said Captain Fowler.

"Isn't magic all illusion?"

"Difficult to tell, missy. That's the wonder of it."

"I'll say one thing about Tate. He seemed more haunted than haunting."

"He's haunting *you*."

"But not scaring me."

"Just the opposite, I'd say."

"I'm more frightened by what I'm about to do," Caroline said.

"You shall not fear the terror by night nor the arrow that flies by day."

"Is that a poem?"

"Psalm ninety-one five. Comforting sailors for a long time."

"I thought it was rum."

"That too," Captain Fowler said with a chuckle. "But it's Christmas Eve—a time for more spiritual things."

"Like a visitant."

~*~

A mile behind the Aegir followed the Mako at the same speed. On the bridge, Lomax watched the lead boat through binoculars and the front window.

"Getting harder to see it," he said, noting the sunset over the left coast.

"He'll run her lights soon," said Yancy Walsh, the shop owner turned pilot of the Mako.

Two minutes later, the Aegir lights came on, deck, pilothouse, and headlight. Lomax turned to Walsh in the darkening bridge.

"What about our lights?"

"No need to show ourselves yet," said Walsh, nodding ahead. "We got us a star to follow."

Lomax pulled a bottle of Molson Ale from the cooler and sat down on the right bench to drink from it. Neither man spoke for a while.

"She's slowing," Walsh said.

He pulled back on the throttle lever to reduce their own speed. Lomax grabbed the binoculars and went to the front window. He watched the Aegir come to a full stop half a mile east of a small island brightened by an antique lighthouse.

"What's that island?" asked Lomax, picking up his cellphone.

"Brighton Rock."

~*~

Peter's mobile rang in the left pocket of his black wool topcoat as he walked out of the Zenith toward the waiting limousine. He raised his right palm to Ramon, about to open the right rear limo door. Ramon waited motionlessly while Peter took the call.

"Tell me." Listening to Lomax, Peter fumed. "Brighton Rock.... Tate.... Are you armed?.... Good.... It may come to that."

He hung up and climbed into the limousine. Ramon closed the door behind him.

Chapter Fourteen

Lomax looked through the binoculars at the Aegir stern deck, watching Captain Fowler and Caroline emerge from the pilothouse. She wore a life vest over her ski outfit and appeared anxious if no less beautiful listening to a somber talk by the captain. She moved to the portside handrail and gazed out at the island, seeming to focus on the old lighthouse. Then she stepped over the handrail. Lomax clutched the binoculars.

"She looks like she's going to—"

Caroline jumped into the sea.

"She jumped," said Lomax.

Caroline started swimming away from the Aegir. On the boat, Captain Fowler observed her for a few seconds then reentered the pilothouse. Caroline got farther away.

"The hell is she doing? Trying to swim to the island?"

"She'll never make it," Walsh said, joining Lomax at the window. "That water's frozen death."

"The old man better pull her out of there quick."

"He will. Stuart Fowler won't let someone die, not even a suicidal nut girl."

The Aegir began moving forward. Lomax switched his view to Caroline, swimming into the dark void left by the distancing boat lights.

"He's not turning around."

"I can't believe it," said Walsh.

Lomax tried to refocus on Caroline but couldn't find her in the dark. The lighthouse beam approaching from the left spotted her for him. Her swim strokes were becoming more erratic, laborious.

"She's losing it," said Lomax.

"Cold's killing her."

The sweeping beam locked on Caroline, revealing her obvious distress.

"The lighthouse guy spotted her," said Lomax.

"What lighthouse guy? That place is totally robotized."

Lomax turned the binoculars to the lighthouse.

"Your call, man," said Walsh. "Whadda you wanna do?"

"Can we save her?"

"No chance. She'll be an icicle by the time we get to her."

"Then we wait."

"For what?"

"New instructions," said Lomax.

He followed the lighthouse beam back to Caroline, now barely moving in the water. But something else was, from the island side, heading fast toward her. Lomax turned his sights to the approaching movement. It was a golden sail attached to a small sailboat. A lone man sat in the back, tacking against the wind, tall and robust in a white knit sweater beneath his square jaw and thick dark hair.

Bobbing in the minor waves, Caroline saw him too and smiled. She mouthed a one-syllable word. Walsh voiced it.

"Tate," he said in awe, joining Lomax at the front window.

"Who is that?"

"Heard talk about 'im. Never bought it. Won't start now. Just a stranger on a boat."

~*~

The sailboat stopped right beside Caroline. Tate grabbed hold of her lifejacket with both hands and pulled her out of the water. He laid her on her back in the front of the boat, just like the first time. She appeared more alive and alert than she had then. Removing her lifevest, Tate felt a bulk inside her drenched ski coat. He pulled the zipper down halfway, exposing the black thermal wetsuit underneath. He looked inquisitively at Caroline, she knowingly at him.

"I'm no fool," she said.

"I am."

Tate left Caroline lying in front and took the

single seat behind the tiller. He maneuvered the stick, changing the angle of the sail so that it caught the inbound wind. Caroline upraised herself to get a better view of him handling the tiller while steering the boat toward Brighton Rock. He looked back at her with apprehension.

"You don't know what you've done," he said.

"What I had to do to find you again."

"Why, Caroline?"

"To make sure you're real."

"But, I'm not."

"You are to me," said Caroline.

Tate's expression remained grim, but Caroline thought she saw his eyes soften. It may have been the splashing saltwater.

Chapter Fifteen

Peter gazed out the rear window of the Harbor Yacht Club at the row of luxury boats and the starlit ocean beyond. He stood apart from the other banqueters with a half-full champagne flute in his hand. Hard as he tried, he couldn't be officially cheerful, knowing she was out there in search of another man.

"You okay, Mr. Fleming?" asked a husky female voice with a slight Southern accent.

Peter turned to a lovelier sight than the harbor, Lisa Holloway, the young blonde tax associate at the firm. She had on a short black cocktail dress with a plunging neckline and a right thigh slit, showing even more shapely leg. She held a champagne glass close to her ample bosom.

"You look kind'a gloomy."

"Distant thoughts," said Peter.

"Anything I can do to have 'em join the party?"

"Not right now."

"Are you sure, Mr. Fleming?"

"It's Christmas Eve, Lisa. You can call me Peter."

"Peter," Lisa said appreciatively.

"How'd you like your first year with our firm?"

"I loved it. Everyone's been so nice."

"What, even me?"

"'Specially you," said Lisa, slinking closer to Peter.

"Well then, I guess I'll have to give you extra work in the New Year."

Lisa smiled.

Peter's cellphone rang. He plucked it out of his suit pants pocket, checking the caller ID. "Pardon me," he said to Lisa.

She sashayed enticingly away as he spoke into the phone.

"Where are you? ... What? ... What?! ... No. Stay put. I'll pay the triple overtime. ... Call me back."

Peter hung up but gripped the phone and began scrolling through his contact numbers.

~*~

Lieutenant William Royce left the examination area looking tired in his uniform overcoat. Soft Christmas music played in the waiting lobby, empty at last. He gave a small wave to Nurse Jill behind the reception desk.

"Merry Christmas, Jill, to you and your large brood."

"It's a lot more peaceful here," said Jill.

Royce smiled as his cellphone rang. Checking the caller ID, he seemed to draw a mental blank but still took the call.

"Hello?.... Oh, of course, Mr. Fleming. How's Miss York?" He stiffened at the reply. "Are you sure?!.... Dangerous? Not to your fiancée. She should be quite safe with him.... No, let us handle it. I'll call you later. Goodbye."

Royce hung up, frowning. Jill noted the change in him. "Bad news, Doctor?"

"Good news for Commander Talbot. He's been waiting a long time for it." Royce pressed a key on his mobile and got a response. He spoke into the phone. "Commander? Your White Whale's been spotted ... Brighton Rock."

Chapter Sixteen

Tate steered the sailboat into the cove with Caroline sitting up in front. Six yards from the beach, he leapt into the knee-high yet powerful current and pulled the craft ashore. He reached down to Caroline with both hands, took her wrists, and effortlessly raised her to her feet. His hands moved to her waist, and he lifted her over the strake to the sand. Tate held her for a moment longer than helpful while studying her face in the lighthouse glow. She smiled encouragingly at him. Her smile appeared to pain him. Suddenly letting go of her, he strode away on the path between the twin boulders.

Caroline hurried after him. Halfway to the lighthouse, she came up behind him. He didn't acknowledge her or slow down until he reached the oak door, which he pulled open by the brass ring and entered the lighthouse ahead of her. Stung by his uncharacteristic lack of gallantry, Caroline followed him inside.

Tate said nothing as he yanked the door shut, appearing lost in thought. He moved past Caroline to the spiral stairwell and began swiftly climbing the steps. She did the same, although at a much slower pace that decreased the higher she rose. On a middle flight, she stopped to catch her breath, looking out the paneless window at the hostile sea. "The Twelve Days of Christmas" began playing faintly above her, and she resumed her stairwell ascent. By the time she reached the den, the song was on the ninth day of Christmas, with nine ladies dancing.

The room felt colder than before. Caroline noticed the electric fireplace was off, and the bare Christmas mini-tree was back on the mantelpiece. This gladdened her strangely. She didn't see Tate right away but then spotted him outside on the deck, adjusting the telescope eyepiece. She slid open the glass door and joined him, now looking through the telescope. She assumed he was deliberately ignoring her, and it hurt.

"Tate, I—"

"You were followed."

"What?"

"Take a look."

Tate stepped aside from the telescope. Caroline took his spot and peered into the eyepiece. She could clearly see the Aegir speeding back to her jump-off point.

"That's just Captain Fowler making sure I'm not still in the ocean," she said. "In which case, he'd've pulled me out, according to the plan."

"Your plan worked. You tricked me. Now they know I'm here."

"Who does?"

"Look right."

Caroline swiveled the telescope slowly to the right and focused on a sight—an aluminum workboat floating in place, its lights on. She recognized it.

"I've seen that boat," she said. "In Kittery. The Mako."

"She followed yours, a mile behind, same speed. Stopped when you stopped."

"Who's on it?"

"You tell me."

"Peter," Caroline said, turning to Tate. "My fian—boyfriend. Someone who works for him."

"Your boy's got trust issues. This won't be a merry Christmas Day."

"I'm sorry, Tate."

"Doesn't matter. I'll be somewhere else by morning—and something else."

Caroline swallowed. The moment of truth had arrived. Did she really want to hear it?

"What do you mean?"

"I'm finishing a job tonight," Tate said with a hint of melancholy. "Kind of a five-year internship. The time has come for my—promotion."

"To Christmas spirit."

Tate flinched. "You know?"

Caroline nodded, amazed by her own calmness. "You're a legend of the sea, Tate. As told by Captain Fowler. Naturally, I had my doubts, but you just dispelled them."

"I see."

"Can you, uhm, talk about it?"

"Why not."

"Thought there might be rules against that sort of thing."

"I never got the rulebook," said Tate. "But first, you'd better get out of that wetsuit and into some dry clothes before you lower my lifesaving average."

"Mrs. Eckstrom's wardrobe will need restocking after my regular visits here."

Tate half smiled.

"Promise me you won't dematerialize, or whatever it is you do, while I'm in the shower."

"I can't 'whatever,'" said Tate, somber again. "I'm still mostly human, till my crossing."

"How will that transpire?"

"I'm not sure. Sir Gareth will guide me through it."

"Ah, your mentor."

"Yeah, Gareth of Orkney. He's been what I'm going to be for a thousand years."

"When does he turn up?"

"Dawn. Christmas Day. 'Bout four hours from now. I'd planned to spend tonight getting ready for it."

"No one should spend Christmas Eve alone," said Caroline.

"I won't have much choice from now on."

"Well, that leaves us tonight."

"For what?"

"Getting better acquainted."

Tate perked up for a moment, then deflated just as quickly. "We may have to cut it short," he said, pointing at the ocean. "Don't forget your friend out there. He won't forget us."

"You're right. Can you drink alcohol in your present state?"

"Yeah. I've had a few the last five years. They don't seem to affect me anymore."

"Will you join me in one?"

"Sure. What would you like?"

"Eggnog."

"Eggnog?!" Tate winced.

"I'm a holiday traditionalist."

"Okay," said Tate. "But you'll have to restock the liquor cabinet too after I'm gone."

Caroline smiled. She slid open the door and went inside. Tate observed her through the door glass until she entered the bathroom, then shook his head. Relooking through the telescope, he saw the Aegir approaching the Mako at top speed.

Chapter Seventeen

The Aegir slowed to a stop on the starboard side of the Mako, facing the opposite direction, south. Captain Fowler exited the pilothouse to the bow just as Yancy Walsh emerged on the Mako stern, accompanied by Lomax. They moved to within vocal range of the Aegir.

"Need help, Yancy?" Captain Fowler inquired.

"No thanks," said Walsh. "All's well."

"You haven't moved for over an hour."

"We're whale watching."

"This late on Christmas Eve? Has to be Moby Dick."

"A job's a job," said Walsh. "And what you doing out here, Stuart?"

"Oh, my new hobby—photography. Was taking some pictures of Brighton Rock."

"On Christmas Eve."

"Sure. Might make a nice Christmas card next year. Can I come aboard?"

Walsh and Lomax went into a huddle, observed by Captain Fowler. Walsh seemed to ask Lomax a couple of questions, to which the other man gave short answers. Walsh turned to Captain Fowler and nodded. He grabbed the rope line and threw the coil to the Aegir. Captain Fowler pulled his boat closer to the Mako and jumped on board.

He cursorily shook hands with Walsh while appraising the other man. Lomax looked formidable. Captain Fowler noted the slight bulge on his sheepskin coat near the right rib as if made by a shoulder holster. Walsh introduced him.

"My customer, Frank Lomax."

Lomax and the captain exchanged nods.

"Got any beer?" Captain Fowler asked.

"Ale," said Walsh.

"That'll do."

Walsh led him toward the pilothouse, followed by Lomax. Captain Fowler noticed the wooden skiff at the starboard edge, ready for a shallow water beach landing.

~*~

Fifty miles north, on the wharf behind the Portland Coast Guard Station, one of two patrol boats was being readied for possible combat. A burly seaman greased the prow-mounted machine gun. A pair of sidearmed seamen stood on the stern while, portside, Seaman Wayne Smith inflated the same raft he'd piloted to Brighton Rock. Two seamen bearing MI6 rifles approached the boat from the short pier.

A blue Ford Fiesta pulled up to the dock, driven by a pretty, pregnant, twentyish brunette. Ensign Tim Bailey sat in the passenger seat. Both observed the patrol boat bustling with martial activity, the woman more anxiously than the ensign.

"I thought you said this was a rescue mission," she said.

"It is. The extra arms are just a precaution."

"Against what—pirates?"

"The unknown," Ensign Bailey said a little somberly.

"What do you mean?"

"I wish I knew, Sandy."

"Well, you'd better come home tomorrow. It's bad enough spending Christmas Eve all by myself."

Ensign Bailey gently placed his left hand on his wife's round belly. "You got company, honey. And you always will from now on."

Sandy smiled sweetly while Ensign Bailey undid his seatbelt. He gave her a kiss on the lips and got out of the car. The patrol boat motor started just as he climbed on board. The four seamen astern saluted him. He returned their salute and continued into the bridge. Seaman Smith stood at attention behind the mariner's wheel.

"Cast off, Wayne," Ensign Bailey said. "Heading—Brighton Rock."

Smith took hold of the throttle lever and pushed it forward. The boat moved out to sea.

Chapter Eighteen

Caroline emerged from the bedroom in an older woman's green flannel dress, her hair still moist from the shower. She sat down on the sofa and watched the false flame flickering once more in the phony fireplace, though its heat was real. Her wet ski suit lay drying in front of it. "The Carol of the Bells" played softly on the sound system.

Tate exited the kitchen, holding two glasses of eggnog. He handed one to Caroline. They clinked glasses in a toast.

"Merry Christmas, Jack," said Caroline.

Tate barely winced, but she saw it.

"Was it something I said?"

"My first name, right after 'Merry Christmas,'" said Tate. "Sounded so natural, like it always did. It'll never be again, 'cause I'll be unnatural."

Caroline swallowed, not yet ready to directly address the mystery. She pointed to the tiny barren Christmas tree on the mantle.

"That sad little tree almost gave you away. You took it with you when you abandoned me."

"I hid it among the rocks," said Tate, stepping to the fireplace. "I kept one in each of the lighthouses I haunted over the last five years."

"All naked like that one?"

"Yeah. I left them that way as a grim reminder of Christmas. How I blew it for good. A decked out tree would've been false advertising."

Caroline realized she could no longer avoid the elephant in the room. "Where'd you go after you ditched me? In fact, where are you the whole year, when you're not out saving souls at Yuletide?"

Tate looked uneasy. "I'm not really sure," he said. "The night I jumped off that cliff, as I sank into the cold black water, this glow appeared deep below me, like a light out of a pit. I had a fast choice to make. Go back up to the surface and get arrested, or down to my probable death, which is what I did, straight into the light. I wound up in a cave, in a land of ice and snow and perpetual twilight. But it's warm inside. There's a bed and a table with two chairs. Out of the cave mouth, I can see ghostly figures darting by, on their way to God knows where. And I know that soon I'll be one of them, unable to touch things—or people." He looked sadly at Caroline. "The only person I ever speak to is Gareth. He brings me food and water while I still need 'em."

"What do you two talk about?"

"Our pasts mostly. He's got mine beat. You know he was a Knight of the Round Table? It really existed, King Arthur and his crew. Fighting evil knights and wizards, and rescuing damsels in distress."

"You did all right on that score," said Caroline.

"He did say one thing that cheered me up. That I couldn't've saved Gus or the others, even if I'd been on the rescue boat."

"Then you're off the hook," Caroline said hopefully.

Tate shook his head. "The Coast Guard couldn't know that. They'll still hang me."

"Right."

"No way out."

"There might be," said Caroline. "What was Gus's request?"

"What?"

"The, ah, boon, he asked on your behalf."

Tate stared at Caroline. "Captain Fowler mentioned that?"

"Yep."

"I can't tell you," said Tate. "Not you."

The emphasis intrigued Caroline. "Why not me?"

Tate grimaced. "You shouldn't've come back, Caroline. I was ready to meet my fate—leave my human form behind. You've made this a lot harder for me."

"I'm sorry," said Caroline, taken aback.

"You know, in a way, it's a more fitting punishment with you here."

"Care to explain that?"

"Pretty women got me into this mess, my shallow view of them. They were easy to hit and run. But you…. You're like their avatar or something—of what could've been if I'd been a better man."

Caroline felt for him. "You're young, Tate. You'd've changed, found someone special."

"I did, just too late."

"Who?"

"You."

Caroline gulped.

"The irony sucks," said Tate.

Caroline leaned back on the sofa, trying to think. Something came out of the effort.

"Look, Tate. I'm new to this whole mystic realm. But if there's any earthly logic to it, it seems to me any 'destiny points' you've earned would include saving me. That's got to count for something in the grand scheme of things.

The least I can do is stay with you till Sir Gareth shows up. Try to put in a good word for you."

"Out of gratitude."

"There's that, and more," said Caroline.

Tate looked inquiringly at her. "What else?"

"Ask me in the morning."

Tate's expression softened. He sat down on the sofa beside Caroline, and they took a simultaneous sip of eggnog, Caroline clearly enjoying hers more than Tate did his.

"Mmm. Just the right touch of cinnamon. Well done, Tate."

"Bartending paid for college," said Tate.

"School? Major?"

"NYU, Archaeology. I plan—planned to be an underwater treasure hunter. It's why I joined the Coast Guard—to learn deep-sea diving while getting paid for it."

"I may not be Blackbeard's chest," said Caroline. "But, I'm glad you salvaged me."

"Your value is beyond pearls."

"Why, thank you, Jack," Caroline said, genuinely enchanted.

A new song started, "Have Yourselves a

Merry Little Christmas," the Judy Garland original.

"And I'll treasure this memory of you for the next thousand years," said Tate.

"Well, we have a little time left to enrich it."

"Then I might as well take the full yield." Tate stood up and extended a hand to Caroline. "May I have this dance?"

Caroline let him pull her to her feet. They began to dance, gracefully at first, then with increasing intimacy. The song lyrics seemed to take on special significance, enhanced by Garland's melancholia.

Have yourself a merry little Christmas. Make the Yuletide gay.

From now on, our troubles will be miles away....

The finale touched their hearts, suggesting that something finer than the dance was ending.

Through the years, we all will be together if the fates allow.

So hang a shining star upon the highest bough.

And have yourself a merry little Christmas now.

They continued to hold each other, faces close until the Pretenders' "2000 Miles" came on.

"Was that the full yield?" Caroline whispered.

"No, this is."

Tate moved his mouth to Caroline's and gave her a fervent kiss. She felt it in more than her lips and reciprocated with them. They kissed for a blissful minute, then Tate pulled away, leaving Caroline yearning for more. He gazed into her eyes.

"I can move on now, with no regrets."

"I don't want you to go, Jack," Caroline said.

"It's all right. You've shown me the real magic of Christmas. What Gus kept trying to teach me."

"Please tell me what he wanted for you."

Tate appeared about to comply but let the moment pass. "I can't," he said.

He put an arm around Caroline's shoulder and walked her to the sofa, where they sat down together. She leaned into him inside his arms circle. He held her shoulder while staring out the glass door at the eastern horizon. Was it getting brighter already?

Chapter Nineteen

Captain Fowler sat on the supply chest in the Mako's bridge, drinking from a bottle of Molson's Dark Ale like the other two men, yet also unlike them. They seemed tenser than he. Walsh sat in the pilot's chair, Lomax in a side seat silently watching the captain while the two sailors conversed. The third beer seemed to be affecting Captain Fowler, slurring his words.

"I saw it eat a polar bear in Uummannaq," he said. "Bear was fishing, sticking his snout into Disko Bay. Damn thing jumps up and bites his head off. His whole head. It was like no shark I'd ever seen before. More of a sea monster." He took another swig of ale.

Lomax and Walsh exchanged quick glances. Walsh addressed Captain Fowler.

"You remember that ghost story you told us at the Anchor Inn a few years back?"

Captain Fowler appeared befuddled, unfocused. "Which one? I spun quite a few of 'em."

"This one had a Christmas twist to it. That's why it crossed my mind. Some Coast Guard kid got turned into a spook, started haunting lighthouses."

"Sounds daffy. I must'a been drunk."

"Not that much," said Walsh. "What was that poor guy's name? Nate?"

Captain Fowler shook his head as if at a loss.

Lomax's cellphone rang. "Yeah," he said. "Locked and loaded. ... Got it. ... Bye." Lomax hung up and addressed Walsh. "Coast guard's going in. I'm to make sure nobody gets off that island before they show up."

He and Walsh turned to Captain Fowler with a suspicious look. The captain put down his empty bottle, apparently unaware of the change in their demeanor. "Thanks for the beer," he said, unfocused. "I better get back on my boat, sleep aboard."

"I'll see you off," said Walsh.

"That's all right. I can handle three beers."

"I insist."

Walsh went out the rear door, followed by Captain Fowler, then Lomax behind him. Captain Fowler walked almost dizzily. They passed the skiff on the right before moving starboard. Reaching the low starboard rail, Captain Fowler turned around to see Lomax staring at him as if in deliberation about something.

"So long, gents," he said, still slurring. "Next round's on me in Kittery."

The captain turned his back on the pair and jumped to the Aegir bow deck, almost stumbling where he landed. He untied the connecting rope and tossed it to the Mako. Heading toward the pilothouse, he peripherally watched Walsh and Lomax enter the other.

Once on the bridge, Captain Fowler's stupor

vanished, and he went straight to the supply chest, opened it, and took out the flare pistol. Moving behind the steering wheel, he restarted the boat engine. He drove the Aegir forward twenty yards past the Mako and stopped.

He walked out to the stern deck holding the flare gun and crossed to the back handrail. Pistol raised, he took steady aim at the skiff on the Mako deck, clearly visible in the pilothouse light. He pulled the trigger. The flare shot across the water and blasted the wooden skiff, setting it ablaze. By the time Walsh and Lomax ran out of the pilothouse, Lomax clutching a grey Ruger pistol, the skiff had burned to junk. They turned from it to the Aegir, now an unreachable distance away.

Captain Fowler could see the fury in their faces. He waved the empty flare pistol. "Sorry!" he shouted. "I was inspecting the flare gun, and a wave made it go off! I'll buy you a new skiff at your shop!"

As the men on the Mako fumed, Captain Fowler reentered the bridge. He retook the helm and pushed forward the throttle. The boat began to move with increasing speed.

"Good luck, mermaid," Captain Fowler said, then broke into song.

"As I was out walkin' down Paradise Street,
To me way, hey, blow the man down!
A pretty young damsel I chanced for to meet
Give me some time to blow the man down!"

The Aegir continued south at sixteen knots, leaving the Mako far behind.

Chapter Twenty

At a quarter past four on Christmas morning, Peter sat on his living room sofa half asleep with his power tie loosened, a near empty glass of vodka in hand, his suitcoat on his lap. It could have been Lisa Holloway, he mused. He had again rebuffed her at the banquet from coming home with him, preferring to be tormented by Caroline for some damnable reason, like love.

The cellphone ring snapped him fully awake. Peter grabbed the instrument.

"Are you on the island?" he asked. The answer enraged him. "What?!.... What about the boat you're on?!.... Then swim there, you son of a—!…. You're fired!"

He hung up, then pressed a preset number. The other line rang several times before he got a response.

"Linda…. Yeah, yeah, Merry Christmas. Listen, I need the helicopter on the roof in half an hour…. I don't care. Tell Joe it'll be his last Christmas with the firm if he can't do it. … Call me back."

He clicked off and stood up. Hurrying to the foyer closet, he withdrew his coat and donned it on his way out the door.

Ramon dropped him off at his office building shortly before five. He entered the lobby, Christmas Muzak playing. He surprised the sleepy desk guard, who sat up straight in his chair.

"Mr. Fleming. Working late on Christmas?"

Peter ignored the question. "There'll be a helicopter landing in five minutes if anyone asks about the noise."

"I doubt they will. There's no one else here."

Peter stepped into an open elevator.

"Merry Christmas to you too, jerk," the

guard said under his breath.

Peter walked out the rooftop door and looked out over downtown Boston. He watched an aerial light draw closer, growing from a firefly to a sleek silver Robinson R-44 Raven II corporate helicopter. It landed nine yards in front of him, a lean, bald man at the control. The blades slowed but kept whirling as Peter mounted the aircraft, with room for two more.

The helicopter lifted off, flying northeast toward the ocean. Peter, sullen in the right window seat, took little notice of the sliver of sunlight peeking over the horizon.

Chapter Twenty-One

Tate watched the brightening horizon. He sat on the couch, looking out the window glass with his right arm around Caroline, a position made easier by her head on his shoulder. She had not yet noticed the light change while recounting her life story over a female version of "What Child Is This."

"And even though my college newspaper column was pretty silly, all about the trials and tribulations of my Wellesley sisters, it got me a job offer from *Max News*."

"Because you're beautiful," said Tate, adding diplomatically, "As well as talented."

Caroline smiled. "That may have had something to do with it. But I really wanted to hone my craft, so I went with the *Boston Globe*, and I still ended up on the fluff page. After two years, I moved to *Sublime* for a lot more money. Now I find the best story of all time, and I can't write it."

"Why not?"

"Two reasons. First, no one will believe it. Second, I can't be objective."

"How come?"

"I'm too close to the subject," said Caroline.

She moved her mouth toward Tate's. Their lips met in a passionate kiss. In mid ecstasy, Caroline glanced out the window and froze, dawn's early light now apparent to her. Tate pulled his head back, his hands still on Caroline's temples.

"Caroline."

"Don't say it," she pleaded. "Please."

"It's happening. Time for me to go."

"No."

"You should go downstairs. Make this easier for me."

"I won't leave you, Jack. You'll have to leave me."

"I've got no choice. Wish to God I did!"

"Maybe I can change things."

"You already have," Tate said. "You taught me the meaning of love. I know how corny that sounds. Three days ago, I would've laughed at the cliché. Now it'll stick with me in whatever form I take. Even when I can't touch you — like this." He squeezed Caroline's hand. "I'll be able to feel you somehow."

"So will I, Jack."

The two embraced. An external sound distracted them, of a distant yet loudening motor. They broke apart, looking curiously at one another.

"Doesn't sound very otherworldly," said Caroline.

"It's a mid-size outboard engine. The kind we use on our defender class patrol boats."

Tate jumped to his feet and ran out to the observation deck, leaving the glass door open. Caroline followed him outside and found him looking to the left. She didn't need the telescope to see what he saw — a Coast Guard patrol boat stopping some fifty yards from the lighthouse, with four rifle-armed seamen astern.

"Does this alter your fate?" she asked.

"Might take me back to square one."

"You'd stay human."

"But in prison for life," said Tate. "Of no use to anyone, like Gareth said. And worst of all, locked away from you."

On their side of the patrol boat, the raft dropped to the water. Two Coast Guardsmen started climbing down to it.

"You'd get a trial," said Caroline.

"A court martial."

"It could go our way."

"Not with Talbot. He'll bury me alive. Either way, I lose you. Being human would hurt more."

The raft began a rapid approach to the island, six Coast Guardsmen on board.

"They'll find your sailboat," said Caroline.

"They won't find me."

The launch disappeared into the cove.

Tate and Caroline turned to each other, she

misty eyed.

"Jack."

"I learned one thing the hard way," said Tate. "Christmas is a sacred time on both sides of the barrier. If there's any way at all, I'll contact you when it comes around one of these years."

"I'll know the sign."

A male voice on the ground floor yelled, "Go!" indicating the oak door was open and men already up the stairwell.

Tate stroked Caroline's cheek. "It's all been worth it, Caroline—all my mistakes, and the price I'm paying for 'em—to love you."

"For one night."

"Forever," Tate said.

He kissed Caroline on the lips with full reciprocation from her. He broke off the kiss and climbed over the guardrail. Caroline heard heavy nearing footsteps from the stairwell behind her, but her eyes never left Tate.

Ensign Bailey popped into the den with a Beretta pistol in hand. He looked through the open door at the two people on the deck. A man stood in front of Caroline, facing the sea, hands spread, and shockingly outside the handrail.

Tate made a perfect dive off the deck. Caroline watched him drop over a hundred feet toward some rocks, clear them, and plunge into the churning surf to disappear from view. Searching the dark waters for him, she became aware of Ensign Bailey on her right, also gaping down at the ocean.

Two seamen came out of the stairwell, ready to storm the deck. Ensign Bailey spun to them. "Stand down!" The pair in the den relaxed, as did their subsequent two reinforcements. Ensign Bailey resumed scanning the sea below. "He couldn't've survived that."

"Stranger things have happened," said Caroline. "A lucky wave might've caught him and borne him to safety."

Ensign Bailey blinked. "My apologies, ma'am. Guess I was wrong about that scenario."

Caroline nodded at the water. "And him."

"Yes. In my defense, though, it wasn't my idea. It was pushed on me by the brass."

"Commander Talbot," said Caroline.

"The word did come down from him. In

any case, I'll correct my report. Do you need a boat ride?"

"No, thank you, Ensign. I think I'll stick around here a while longer."

"Ma'am," Ensign Bailey said, putting extra deference into the word.

He went into the den. All four seamen looked expectantly at him. "Let's clear out."

The seamen started down the stairwell. Ensign Bailey took a last look at Caroline on the deck, still staring down at the water, and descended after his men.

~*~

An instrumental version of "The First Noel" started playing on the sound system. Caroline barely heard it as she scanned the sea and rocks below.

"Seek him not there," said an English-accented male voice in her left ear. "You shan't find him."

Caroline was unsurprised by her lack of surprise. Turning left, she saw exactly what she expected to see — an imposing man in a crimson hooded cloak, with a goatee on his handsome face, standing beside her.

"Sir Gareth of Orkney," she said.

Gareth bowed to her in an archaic manner. "At your service, Lady Caroline."

"You know my name."

"How could I not? I heard it oft enough o'er the past three days from my heir apparent."

Caroline smiled slightly. "Where is he?" she asked.

"In the grotto, awaiting the verdict of the High Judge on his destiny."

"I thought it'd been decided. He'll be a Christmas spirit like you for the next thousand years."

"Twas the idea. But a plea by his good comrade has caused a stir."

"Gus," said Caroline. "The boon request."

"Indeed."

"What was it?"

Gareth looked at Caroline in surprise. "You truly do know not?"

"No, Jack wouldn't tell me."

Gareth seemed impressed. "'Tis to his credit. He hath changed for the good. That may sway the judge."

"Tell me, Gareth. What did Gus ask for Tate?"

"That given one improbable occurrence, he would remain mortal."

"What occurrence?"

"Should he find true love 'ere he cross the bar."

Caroline gripped the handrail, observed by Gareth.

"Did he?" he asked.

"Yes," said Caroline. "That he did."

"Ah. So Simon was right."

"Simon?"

"A good comrade of mine. He blows the most peculiar trumpet."

"The saxophonist by the subway station," said Caroline.

"'Twas he. I asked him to appraise you. He said you were in love."

"He knew before I did."

"I must remark, my lady, that Tate was blessed to find you."

"And I him," said Caroline.

"Then good fortune to you both, and Happy Christmas."

Gareth turned around and started walking away on the deck.

"Wait," said Caroline. "What about the judgment?"

"If you hear naught, then the boon was denied."

Gareth continued walking on the circular deck until he disappeared around the lighthouse curve.

A vocal rendition of "Joy to the World" emanated from the den, but Caroline heard something more, another loudening engine. Turning right, she saw helicopter lights rushing over the ocean toward the lighthouse. She recognized the wide cockpit as something she'd been in once, on a flight to New York with Peter. She moved into the den, sliding the glass door shut.

The helicopter landed fairly close to the lighthouse door. Caroline exited through it, wearing her now nearly dry ski suit. Peter got out of the aircraft and signaled the pilot to reduce the motor. He met Caroline halfway from the lighthouse and hugged her tightly. She returned the embrace less intensely. Peter unhanded her.

"You had me followed," said Caroline.

"I was worried about you."

"No, you didn't trust me—and with good reason."

Caroline said the last part kindly, which appeared to sting Peter worse.

"You said there wasn't another man," he said.

"There wasn't, then. Merely the ghost of one."

"Ghost?"

"Of Christmas Past. Christmas Future may be more corporeal. I dearly hope so."

"You're not making any sense, Caroline."

"Aren't I? Perhaps I'm still in a state of shock."

Peter ignored the barb. "Where's your lighthouse keeper?"

"Vanished again. It's his way."

"Now yours," Peter said bitterly. "Am I

right?"

Caroline slipped the engagement ring off her left hand and handed it to him. "I'm sorry, Peter. You deserve better."

"True," he said. "But finding her won't be easy."

Caroline smiled wanly. Peter turned to the helicopter and signaled the pilot to get ready for takeoff. He turned back to Caroline. "Want a lift back to Boston?"

"How about halfway there, to Kittery?"

"Captain Fowler."

"He's sailing for Greece today. I'd like to say goodbye and thank him."

"Don't thank him for me," said Peter.

Even he chuckled at that, along with Caroline. He escorted her into the helicopter. It lifted off right away, flying southwest toward the mainland.

Chapter Twenty-Two

Caroline stepped off the revving helicopter at the broad end of Main Street in the holiday empty marina. She noted the "closed" sign on the door of Yancy's Marine Supplies and Boat Charters and began walking rapidly by the row of boats on her left. She heard then saw the helicopter buzz over her head and past the row of boats, taking Peter out of her life.

She paused before the Mako, curious about its involvement in last night's adventure, but let it pass and resumed her walk. She reached the Aegir, the only vessel around with any visible activity aboard. On the stern deck, a young blond crewman in a grey wool sweater lowered a fire extinguisher into the open hatch, from where arose two massive black arms to take it down. A female version of "Do You Know Where Christmas Trees Are Grown?" emanated from the pilothouse. It got louder when the back door opened, and Captain Fowler came out. He closed the door behind him, dulling the song. He saw Caroline and grinned.

"Request permission to come aboard," she said.

"Ted, give the lady a hand."

The young crewman assisted Caroline onto the deck. Captain Fowler peered into the open hatch.

"How's it looking down there, Nat?"

"Good till Lisbon, Skipper," said a deep voice from below.

Captain Fowler nodded cheerfully. Crewman Ted began separating a tall stack of folded aluminum chairs into two shorter stacks. For the Harvard tour students, Caroline deduced. She turned to Captain Fowler.

"Aren't you going to ask me how it went?"

"I have a pretty good idea. But I was going to look you up in Beantown tonight. We'll be picking up fresh food there for tomorrow's ocean crossing."

"Oh good, then you won't mind a passenger."

"This is a working vessel, missy. You'll have to earn your fare home."

"How?"

"Assisting my new first mate in the messroom. He's doubling as our bartender. Insists on making foo-foo drinks." Captain Fowler cringed. "Like eggnog."

Caroline stared at him and thought she saw a twinkle in his blue eye. She rushed into the pilothouse, feeling her heartbeat quicken even over the now louder Christmas song. The door to the lower deck was ajar. She went through it and down the steep staircase.

Pivoting left at the doorless first compartment and standing just outside it, she took in the compact dining room, six-seat table, and kitchenette. She saw something on top of the mini-refrigerator that had not been there the night before. It was a tiny Christmas tree, fully ornamented. She took a deep breath and entered the compartment.

A high open cabinet displayed bottles of rum, wine, Scotch, and beer. In front of it, with his back to her, stood a muscular man in a black sailor cap, black T-shirt, and blue jeans, writing on a flip notebook. Suddenly his hand stopped as if in mid-word, and he turned to her. Caroline gasped, looking at Tate, and he at her. An incalculable moment later, she was in his arms, kissing him and being kissed, either way delightful.

"You're human, Jack!" gushed Caroline. "Flesh and blood and wonderful!"

"I never thought I'd feel your lips again," Tate said.

"They're yours forever."

"Minus nine-hundred years or so."

Caroline laughed joyously.

"Believe me, I'm grateful for the time limit," said Tate.

Caroline got a worried thought. "Wait, what are we gonna do? You're a wanted man."

"No, I'm a dead man, officially, after my dashing lighthouse leap. And a year on the Aegean will make me even deader. A lot of sunken ships lie under that sea, dating back to Ancient Greece. Profitable work for a treasure hunter. Enough to enrich a happy marriage."

Caroline smiled, then mock scowled. "And what will your lovely bride be doing for a whole year, besides worrying about you being eaten by a shark?"

"Ah," said Tate. "I know a grizzled sea captain who needs help writing a book, all about fantastic happenings. And one with a fairy tale ending."

Caroline smiled. "Could be a best seller, with the right ghostwriter."

"Better you than me," said Tate.

They both laughed and kissed again as the song from the upper deck went into its finale.

Do you know how Christmas cards are made?
They need pictures and greetings,
Sunshine and raindrops,
Snowflakes and reindeer,
Friendship and kindness,

And most of all, they need love.

About the Author

Lou Aguilar was born in Cuba and lived there until age six, when his anti-Castro scholar father flew the family to America one step ahead of a firing squad (for his dad, not him). He attended the University of Maryland, where he majored in English, minored in film, and found both to be dependent on great writing. He became a journalist for *The Washington Post* and *USA Today*, then a produced screenwriter then an established novelist.

His debut book, *Jake for Mayor*, came out in 2016 to glowing reviews. His controversial second novel, *Paper Tigers*, was published Christmas 2019. Lou is a frequent arts and literature opinionist for the American Spectator (https://spectator.org/author/lou-aguilar/). Lou is single, having postponed marriage until he made the *New York Times* bestsellers list. So buy this book for the sake of romance.

Made in the USA
Columbia, SC
20 December 2020